The Virgins

by Miriam Battye

The Virgins was first performed at Soho Theatre, London, on 29 January 2026

THE VIRGINS
by Miriam Battye

Cast

Anya   Zoë Armer
Mel   Alec Boaden
Jess   Ella Bruccoleri
Chloe   Anushka Chakravarti
Phoebe Molly Hewitt-Richards
Joel   Ragevan Vasan

Director   Jaz Woodcock-Stewart
Set and Costume Designer   Rosie Elnile
Lighting Designer   Bethany Gupwell
Sound Designer   Anna Clock
Casting Director   Polly Jerrold
Intimacy Director   Raniah Al-Sayed
Costume Supervisor   Megan Rarity
Assistant Director   Rute Costa
Production Manager   Davin Patrick for The Production Family
Production Wellbeing Support   Tricia Gannon for Artist Wellbeing Company
Production Assistant for Soho Theatre   Daljinder Johal
Producer for Soho Theatre   Eve Allin
Executive Producer   David Luff

Company Stage Manager   Roisin Symes
Deputy Stage Manager   Jodie Jasmin Hicks
Assistant Stage Manager   Daze Corder

Cast and Creative Team

Zoë Armer (Anya)

Zoë graduated from LAMDA in 2021.

Her theatre credits include *The Suppliant Women* (Manchester Royal Exchange – Community Ensemble), *Gargantua* (Salford Lowry – NT Connections), *On Songbirds' Wings* (Bolton Octagon Young Company) and *Zigger Zagger* (Wilton's Music Hall – National Youth Theatre)

Her screen credits include *So Awkward* (CBBC), *Casualty* (BBC), *Emmerdale* (ITV) and *EastEnders* (BBC), as well as independent films: *Kind Hearts and Cornettos* (Jade Jones), *Truth Serum* (Vika Evdokimenko), *Voidance* (Marianna Dean) and *Misconceptions* (Marianna Dean).

The Virgins marks her professional stage debut.

Alec Boaden (Mel)

Alec is a native Nottingham actor and a recent graduate of Guildhall School of Music & Drama. Before graduating, Alec was cast in his first professional theatre production, James Graham's *Punch* (4**** in the *Guardian* & the *Telegraph*), which transferred to the Young Vic in London and has now opened in the West End. Alec also recently played a supporting lead in the stage adaptation of Malorie Blackman's novel *Noughts + Crosses* at Regent's Park Open Air Theatre.

Alec trained from a young age at Nottingham's prestigious Television Workshop. His television credits include *Masters of the Air* on Apple TV+.

Ella Bruccoleri (Jess)

Ella has recently wrapped on the lead role of Mary Bennet in the upcoming BBC/Britbox period drama *The Other Bennet Sister*.

Recent film credits include *Bank of Dave 2*, *Paddington in Peru* and Netflix's *Joy*.

Ella has extensive credits across film and television including the new horror trilogy *The Strangers*, BBC's *Call the Midwife*, ITV's *Passenger* and *The Chelsea Detective*, BBC's *Ludwig*, Disney+'s *Extraordinary*, Netflix's *The Last Kingdom* and the third series of *Bridgerton*, as well as Alibi's *Bookish*.

She recently wrapped as the lead role opposite Hugh Bonneville and Michael Socha in the comedy feature *Go Away!* Ella can currently be seen as a series regular in Apple's *Down Cemetery Road* and in 2026, look out for the indie feature *Wicker* with Olivia Colman, Elizabeth Debicki and Alexander Skarsgård.

Anushka Chakravarti (Chloe)

Anushka Chakravarti trained at the Royal Central School of Speech and Drama and studied at Oxford University.

Stage credits include *Poor Clare* (Orange Tree Theatre); *Coriolanus*, *The Crucible* and *Our Generation* (National Theatre) and *The Divine Mrs S* (Hampstead Theatre).

Television credits include *Andor* (Disney+); *Peacock* and *Jerk* (BBC Three); *Never Let Me Go* (Minim UK Productions) and *Call the Midwife* S15 (BBC One, PBS).

Film credits: *Ghostwriter* (Warner Bros. Pictures).

Molly Hewitt-Richards (Phoebe)

Molly Hewitt-Richards trained at Italia Conti.

Stage credits include *A Midsummer Night's Dream* (Bridge Theatre) and *The Secret Garden* (Regent's Park Open Air Theatre).

Television credits include *Code of Silence* (ITV) and *Casualty* (BBC).

Ragevan Vasan (Joel)

Ragevan is a three-time OffWestEnd Awards nominee.

Ragevan can be seen as Felzonis in *Andor* (Disney+) and Gavin in Sky Atlantic's *Save Me*. Other television roles include *Cuffs* (BBC), *Fortitude* (Sky) and *The State* (Channel 4).

His previous theatre credits include *Little Scratch* (New Diorama Theatre and Hampstead Theatre); *The Animal Kingdom* (Hampstead Theatre); *Name, Place, Animal, Thing* (Almeida); *Living Newspaper* (Royal Court); *I Wanna Be Yours* (Bush Theatre); *The Village* (Stratford East); *Love for Love* (RSC) and *Hurling Rubble at the Sun* (Park Theatre).

Ragevan's film credits include *Dumbo* (dir. Tim Burton), *Walk Like a Panther*, *The Last Witness* and *Daphne*.

He trained with the NYT Rep Company.

Miriam Battye – Writer

Miriam Battye is a writer from Manchester.

For theatre, credits include *Strategic Love Play* (Paines Plough/Soho Theatre), *Scenes with girls* (Royal Court) and *Find a Partner!* (NT Connections).

For television, her credits include *Succession* (HBO), *Dead Ringers* (Amazon) and the upcoming *The Husbands* for Apple/A24.

For film, her credits include the upcoming *Extra Geography* for Film4/BFI/Screen Yorkshire.

Jaz Woodcock-Stewart – Director

Jaz is a director working in theatre and screen.

Her production of *Paradise Now!* (Bush Theatre) was nominated for an Olivier Award. She has been nominated for Best Director at the OffWestEnd Awards for her productions of *Multiple Casualty Incident* (Yard Theatre) and *Paradise Now!* (Bush Theatre). Her production *Civilisation* (JWScompany), a collaboration with choreographer Morgann Runacre-Temple, won the Jury Prize at Fast Forward Festival (2021), the European festival for young directors at Dresden Staatschauspiel. It was also selected for Radikal Jung in Munich (2022).

Theatre work as Director includes *Gulliver's Travels* (Deutches National Theater Weimar); *The Glass Menagerie* (Theater Basel); *The Attempts* (JWScompany); *Grud* (Hampstead Theatre); *Multiple Casualty Incident* (Yard Theatre); *Jason Medea Medley* (Dresden Staatschauspiel); *Paradise Now!* (Bush Theatre); *Electric Rosary* (Manchester Royal Exchange); *Gulliver's Travels* (Unicorn); *Civilisation* (UK and international tour); *Something New* (Thomas Bernhard Institut); *Lands* (Bush Theatre); *If I Were Me* (Soho Theatre); *Learning Piece* (The Place); *Days Like This* (BAC/BeFestival).

Selected Associate/Assistant work includes: *Enemy of the People* (Duke of York's); *All About Eve* (Noel Coward); *Network* (National Theatre); *Lazarus* (King's Cross Theatre); *Adler and Gibb* (Royal Court/tour).

She is a Resident this year with House Productions.

She trained on the National Theatre Studio Directors Course, at East 15 Acting School and Dartington College of Arts.

Rosie Elnile – Set and Costume Designer

Rosie Elnile is an award-winning set and costume designer working between theatre, opera and live art.

Her work includes *Die Glasmenagerie* (Staatsschauspiel Basel), *Taming of the Shrew*, *Titus Andronicus* (Shakespeare's Globe); *The Faggots and their Friends Between Revolutions* (Festival d'Aix en Provence); *Jason Medea Medley* (Staatsschauspiel, Dresden); *A fight against, Goat's Primetime* (Royal Court Theatre); *Paradise Now!* (Bush Theatre); *Violet* (Britten Pears Arts); *Prayer, The Ridiculous Darkness, The Unknown Island* and *The Convert* (Gate Theatre); *Our Town* (Regent's Park Open Air Theatre), *The Wolves* (Theatre Royal Stratford East); *The Mysteries* and *Drei Schwestern* (Manchester Royal Exchange); *Abandon* (Lyric Hammersmith) and *Returning to Haifa* (Finborough Theatre).

Bethany Gupwell – Lighting Designer

Bethany Gupwell is a London-based lighting designer, trained at the Royal Central School of Speech and Drama. In 2018, she was awarded the Association of Lighting Designers' Francis Reid Award.

At Soho Theatre: *Little Brother, Brown Girls Do It Too, Mama Told Me Not to Come, Fitter, Wonder Winterland*.

Credits include: *Ohio* (Young Vic); *All's Well That Ends Well* (Shakespeare's Globe); *Larmes de couteau / Full Moon in March* (Royal Opera House); *Escaped Alone / What If Only, Shed: Exploded View* (Manchester Royal Exchange); *Twelfth Night, Quiet Songs, A Play for the Living in a Time of Extinction, Lay Down Your Burdens* (Barbican); *La Voix Humaine* (Opéra National du Rhin); *Dead Woman* (Schaubühne); *Visit from an Unknown Woman, This Much I Know, To Have and to Hold* (2023 Offie nomination), *Little Scratch, Wolf Cub* (Hampstead Theatre); *The Earthworks* (Young Vic); *Robin Hood* (Theatre Royal Bath); *Here, The Woods* (Southwark Playhouse); *Lady Dealer* (Bush Theatre); *War & Culture, Little Scratch, Keep Watching* (New Diorama); *Ignition* (Frantic Assembly); *The Pirate, the Princess and the Platypus* (Polka Theatre); *In Praise of Love, Rice, Little Baby Jesus* (Orange Tree); *Talking Heads* (Watford Palace).

Anna Clock – Sound Designer

Anna Clock (they/them) is a Composer and Sound Artist working across theatre, film, radio and installation. Their audio works have been played on Radio 4, Radio 3, Resonance FM and RTE Lyric radio and presented at venues including the Science Museum, V & A Museum, and Wellcome Collection. They are currently pursuing a funded Doctoral award with the Science Museum exploring how we listen to outer space.

For Soho Theatre: *Mum, Not F**kin' Sorry, Shuck 'n' Jive, Soft Animals, Fabric*.

Theatre credits include *Echo* (Royal Court & World tour); *Hothouse* (Irish Arts Centre NYC; Dublin Fringe Festival); *Joint* (Barbican); *Lay Down Your Burdens* (Barbican & UK tour); *Faith Healer* (Lyric Hammersmith); *Amelia* (Dublin Theatre Festival); *The Duchess of Malfi* (Shakespeare's Globe); *Hynos* (Agit-Cirk, Helsinki); *Jason Medea Medley* (Staatsschauspiel Dresden); *Graceland* (Royal Court); *A Family Business* (China Plate Theatre/Staatstheater Mainz); *Kabul Goes Pop* (Brixton House); *Electric Rosary* (Manchester Royal Exchange); *Faith Healer, The Beauty Queen of Leenane* (Lyric Hammersmith); *Crave* (Chichester Festival Theatre); *A Christmas Carol* (Gate Theatre, Dublin); *Speak, Softly, Go Far* (Digital; Abbey Theatre).

Polly Jerrold – Casting Director

Theatre credits include *The Virgins* (Soho Theatre); *Wolves on Road*, *Paradise Now!* (Bush Theatre); *The Secret Garden*, *Robin Hood*, *Antigone*, *Peter Pan*, *A Tale of Two Cities*, *Oliver Twist*, *To Kill A Mockingbird* tour, *Running Wild* tour (Regent's Park Open Air Theatre); *Earthworks*, *Chasing Hares*, *The Secretaries* (Young Vic); *Private Lives* (Rose Theatre Kingston/Bolton/Northern Stage/Bristol Old Vic); *First Touch* (Nottingham Playhouse); *Life of Pi* (Sheffield Theatres, UK tour & West End); *Silence* (Tara); *Run Rebel* (Pilot); *Tick Tick Boom*, *Snake in the Grass*, *Kill Thy Neighbour*, *Rope*, *Constellations*, *The Great Gatsby*, *Pretty Shitty Love*, *Milky Peaks*, *Celebrated Virgins*, *Curtain Up* and *For the Grace of You Go I* (Theatr Clwyd); *Santi & Naz* (Carbon Theatre); *Shandyland* (Northern Stage); *One Flew Over the Cuckoo's Nest*, *Tribes* (Sheffield Theatres); *Our Lady of Kibeho*, *Soul*, *Merlin*, *Peter and the Starcatcher* (Royal & Derngate); *Macbeth*, *Two Trains Running* (ETT); *Approaching Empty* (Kiln, Tamasha and Live Theatre); *The Lovely Bones* (Royal & Derngate, Birmingham Rep and Northern Stage); *All's Well That Ends Well* (Shakespeare's Globe); *The Caretaker* (Bristol Old Vic); *The Government Inspector*, *Tommy*, *Our Country's Good* (Ramps on the Moon Consortium); *The Island Nation* (Arcola); *Brideshead Revisited*, *A View from the Bridge*, *Sherlock* (York Theatre Royal); *Anita & Me*, *Peter Pan*, *Of Mice and Men*, *A Christmas Carol*, *101 Dalmatians*, *What Shadows*, *Folk*, *Winnie and Wilbur*, *Back Down*, *Feed the Beast*, *I Knew You* (Birmingham Rep); *Waldo's* (Extraordinary Bodies/Bristol Old Vic); *The Kitchen Sink*, *Educating Rita* (Hull Truck Theatre); *Sweet Charity*, *Wit*, *The Ghost Train*, *Little Shop of Horrors* (Manchester Royal Exchange).

Raniah Al-Sayed – Intimacy Director

Raniah comes from an acting background and is now a Movement Practitioner and Intimacy Director, with a specialty in the physical acting process of Lucid Body. She is a faculty member at Shakespeare's Globe Higher Education Department and the senior teacher at Lucid Body London.

Theatre work includes *The Crucible* (Shakespeare's Globe); *Clueless the Musical* (Trafalgar Theatre); *Peaky Blinders: The Rise* (Immersive Everywhere); *Bootycandy* (Gate Theatre); *Multiple Casualty Incident* (The Yard); *£1 Thursdays* (Finborough Theatre); *Supernova* (Theatre503); *The Hypochondriac*, *How a City Can Save the World*, *Fossil Kids* (Sheffield People's Theatre); *Here & Now*, *Now That's What I Call A Musical* (National Tour/ROYO). Upcoming theatre: *Deep Azure* (Shakespeare's Globe).

Film and Television work includes *Hit Point*, *Alize's Room*, *I'm Not Finished*, *The Wife and Her House Husband*, *Salt Wounds*, *Remi Milligan: Lost Director*, *Dreamland* (Assistant I.C.).

Megan Rarity – Costume Supervisor

Megan trained at Arts University Bournemouth in Costume for Performance Design.

Theatre credits include *Mrs President* (Charing Cross Theatre); *Pinocchio The Musical*, *Cymbeline*, *All's Well That Ends Well*, *Ghosts* (Shakespeare's Globe); *Choir* (Chichester Festival Theatre); *The Other Place* (National Theatre); *Macbeth* (Harold Pinter Theatre, Donmar Warehouse); *101 Dalmatians the Musical* (Runaway Entertainment); *Watch on the Rhine* (Donmar Warehouse); *The SpongeBob Musical*, *We Will Rock You!* (Selladoor Worldwide); *Gulliver's Travels* (Unicorn Theatre); *Red Pitch* (Bush Theatre); *Indecent Proposal the Musical* (Southwark Playhouse); *Camp Siegfried* (Old Vic); *The Two Character Play* (Hampstead Theatre); *Shedding a Skin* (Soho Theatre); *The Comeback* (Noël Coward Theatre); *Little Shop of Horrors* (LAMDA); *Cinderella the Musical*, *The Audience*, *A Streetcar Named Desire* (Nuffield Southampton Theatre); *Hedda Gabler* (Sherman Theatre); *Shook* (Southwark Playhouse); *Valued Friends* (Rose Theatre Kingston); *West Side Story* (Hartshorn-Hook Productions); *Ubu Karaoke* (Kneehigh Theatre Company); *Last Easter*, *Blood Knot*, *Utility*, *Mayfly* (Orange Tree Theatre); *Eugenius!* (The Other Palace); *Insignificance* (Arcola); *Oklahoma!* (Bennet Memorial Diocesan School); *Posh* (Pleasance Theatre); *The Tempest* (Coronet Theatre).

Opera credits include *Mazeppa* (Grange Park Opera); *The Elixir of Love, The Rape of Lucretia, What Dreams May Come, The Capulets & The Montagues, The Rake's Progress, Manon Lescaut, The Coronation of Poppea, La Cenerentola* (English Touring Opera); *Cosi Fan Tutte, Orfeo, Rusalka, Turn of the Screw, Der Rosenkavalier, Eugene Onegin* (Garsington Opera Festival).

Film and Television credits include *Britain's Got Talent* (Fremantle Media Ltd); *Festival of Remembrance* (BBC); *Cotton Tail* (Akiko Films Ltd); *The Crown* (Sony Pictures Television).

Davin Patrick for The Production Family – Production Manager

The Production Family deliver a variety of theatre, dance and live experiences in the UK and across the globe. Recent credits: Manchester International Festival, *Museum of Austerity* for English Touring Theatre. Upcoming projects include large-scale immersive touring experiences, *The Other Place* at the Shed, New York, and the Spring season at Soho Theatre.

Rute Costa – Assistant Director

Rute is a Portuguese-born, London-based director and theatre-maker. She has a strong movement-based practice, and a background in literature, dance and activism. She has an MFA in Advanced Theatre Practice from Central and is an alumna of the Stonecrabs Directors in Practice Programme 2022. She is a co-founder of Popsie Theatre, a collective of queer and international artists making politically minded, darkly comedic physical theatre; and of Alento Collective, an interdisciplinary performing arts company making movement and music-driven work.

As director: *Felixxx* (Drayton Arms Theatre); *GEORGE* (Omnibus Theatre); *Mitzi Fitz: Babycakes* (VAULT & The Glory); *Queendom* (Rosemary Branch Theatre); *I am the wind* (Omnibus Theatre); *exile* (also writer, Corpus Playroom & Edinburgh Fringe).

As movement director: *The Dance* (Pushpin music video); *Reigen* (Venue 45, Edinburgh Fringe).

As acting coach: *Clocks* (short film)

As performer/co-creator: *The Triumph of Death* (Theatre Deli & Camden People's Theatre); *Not a Girl Not Yet a Woman* (Blue Elephant & Camden People's Theatre); *ALL YOU NEED IS LOVE?* (Camden People's Theatre).

Tricia Gannon – Production Wellbeing Support

Tricia Gannon began her career as an actor, working in the industry for over twenty years, including with Soho Theatre. Since 2013, she has been a registered Drama and Movement Therapist (HCPC), bringing over twelve years of clinical experience to her practice. Since 2022, she has also been a Clinical Creative Arts Supervisor.

Tricia has worked in both mainstream and special educational settings, with a particular interest in neurodiversity. She provides clinical supervision to senior educational staff and psychotherapy students who work with clients in the creative industries.

As a wellbeing practitioner with The Artist's Wellbeing Company, Tricia is currently working with Soho Theatre, Royal Court, Dan Daw Dance Company, Young Directors Scheme and Space 2 Community Arts. Previous clients include Theatre by the Lake, Stellar Quines Theatre and Cambridge Junction.

Roisin Symes – Company Stage Manager

Roisin Symes is a freelance stage manager.

Recent credits include *The Two Gentleman of Verona*, directed by Joanna Bowman (Royal Shakespeare Company); *The Gift*, directed by Adam Meggido (PostScript Productions at Park

Theatre); *Wuthering Heights*, directed by Lucinka Eisler (China Plate and Inspector Sands at Royal & Derngate; tour) and *A Dead Body in Taos*, directed by Rachel Bagshaw (Fuel Theatre at Wilton's Music Hall; tour).

Jodie Jasmin Hicks – Deputy Stage Manager

Jodie Jasmin Hicks is a freelance Stage Manager from Cambridgeshire. She has worked across a wide range of productions including national tours, pantomimes and in-house productions.

Theatre includes *Even More... Ghost Stories by Candlelight* (UK tour); *MILLENNIUM GIRLS* (Brixton House); *The Gel* (New Diorama); *STILL THE HOURS* (Hampton Court Palace); *Sleeping Beauty* (New Wolsey Theatre); *Luna Loves Library Day The Musical* (UK tour); *Solomon* (JW3/Stanley Arts); *In the Sick of It* (Assembly Rooms, Edinburgh); *Girlhood* (Greenside, Edinburgh); *No More Numbers!* (Mercury Theatre); *Cinderella* (Saffron Hall); *FLOOD* (UK tour); *Beneath the Banner* (UK tour).

Daze Corder – Assistant Stage Manager

Credits include *Scenes from a Repatriation* (Royal Court); *52 Monologues for Young Transsexuals*, *Ugly Sisters* (piss / CARNATION); *UPROOTED*, *Precipice* (New Diorama); *The Ballad of Hattie and James*, *The Purists*, *The Maladies* (Kiln); *Everything I Own* (Sankofa Productions & Brixton House).

David Luff – Executive Producer for Soho Theatre

David Luff is an independent theatre producer who works across the subsidised and commercial sectors. He was Producer, Head of Theatre and Creative Director at Soho Theatre from 2012 to 2025. Notable world premiere productions he produced for Soho Theatre include the Olivier Award-winning *Boys on the Verge of Tears* by Sam Grabiner, directed by James Macdonald; *My English Persian Kitchen* by Hannah Khalil from an original story by Atoosa Sepehr; *Age is a Feeling* by Haley McGee, directed by Adam Brace; *Typical* by Ryan Calais Cameron; and new shows from Kim Noble and Lucy McCormick. Alongside DryWrite, he produced the revivals and world tours of *Fleabag* by Phoebe Waller-Bridge and its New York and West End transfers. With his producing partner Patrick Myles he commissioned and produced the world premiere of *Network* by Lee Hall, directed by Ivo van Hove at the National Theatre before transferring to the Belsaco Theatre on Broadway, winning Olivier and Tony Awards. They subsequently commissioned and produced the world premiere stage adaptation of Stanley Kubrick's *Dr. Strangelove*, adapted by Armando Iannucci and Sean Foley, starring Steve Coogan, playing in the West End and Dublin's Bord Gáis Energy Theatre.

About Soho Theatre

Soho Theatre is London's most vibrant producer of new theatre, comedy and cabaret. A charity and social enterprise, we're driven by a passion for working with bold stories and distinctive artists, connecting them with audiences in original style and creating memorable nights out.

From our early roots in the radical 1970s Soho Poly, we've grown – *and grown* – from a tiny fringe space into a widely influential cultural organisation operating across our four London performance spaces; through international touring and collaborations with India and elsewhere; as festival regulars from Edinburgh Festival Fringe to Melbourne International Comedy Festival; and filming shows and creating our own digital work seen across social platforms and inflight.

Alongside working with some of the most exciting theatre-makers and comedians in the world, we also nurture the next generation of artists through a thriving range of artist and talent development programmes, artists under commission and in development, and two new writing awards including UK's longest established playwriting prize, the Verity Bargate Award.

In 2025 we celebrated 25 years at our central London venue Soho Theatre – described by Phoebe Waller-Bridge as the 'the mothership of new artists', Ryan Calais Cameron as 'a major launchpad' and Bryony Kimmings as 'an extraordinary place for people whose work is genre pushing' – whilst opening London's newest venue, the 'jaw-dropping 1000 seat new theatre' (Time Out), Soho Theatre Walthamstow in May 2025.

sohotheatre.com | @sohotheatre | @sohotheatreindia

Soho Theatre Staff

EXECUTIVE & SENIOR TEAM

CEO & Executive Director
Mark Godfrey

Co-Executive Director
Sam Hansford

Co-Creative Directors
Rose Abderabbani (Theatre Programme),
Steve Lock (Comedy),
Jessica Draper (Creative Engagement)

Co-Audience & Communications Directors
Peter Flynn,
Kelly Fogarty

Fundraising and Partnerships Director
Bhavita Bhatt

Operations Director
Edel McGrath

TRUSTEES

Chair
Dame Heather Rabbatts DBE

Board Members
Nicholas Allott OBE, David Aukin, Farzana Baduel, Lucy Davies, Martin Esom, Hani Farsi, Campbell Glennie, Lornette Harley, Fawn James, Shaparak Khorsandi, Kate Mayne, David Reitman

TEAMS

Executive Assistant
Annie Jones

Assistant to Creative Heads
Lola Ferguson

Theatre Eve Allin, Alessandro Babalola, Max Elton, Pooja Sivaraman, Paul Sirett, Maddie Wilson, Daljinder Johal, Ellen Ritchie

Comedy
Kathryn Craigmyle, Lee Griffiths, Jet Vevers

Creative Engagement
Jenny Bakst, Jules Haworth, Shazad Khalid, Déviniat Adedibu

Press & PR
Augustin Wecxsteen, Ruby Willis, Lou Doyle

Marketing Kia Noakes, Val Londono Cardona, Alicia Bridge, Flo Granger

Graphic design
Conor Jatter, Ludmila Bogatchek

Digital
Rhys Matthews, Laura-Inès Wilson, Jody Davies

Audience & Sales
Mariko Primarolo, Jack Cook, Fuad Ahammed, Lainey Alexander, Kitty Smith, Luke Talboys, Sophie Greaves

Operations
Paul Symes, Gianna Schuetz-McKinnis, Laura Schofield, Em Carr, Dee Lindo, Louisa Pennell, Luca Newman

Technical
Stefan Andrews, Amy Whitby-Baker, Rob Johnson, Ben Goodwin, Tom Younger, Charlie Leslie, Yas Trowbridge, Aidan Walker, Zac Brewin, Lydia Edwards, Finley Dickins

Food & Beverage Scott Viney, Rishay Naidoo, Ronnie Matczuk, Damian Regan, Evan Jones, Nes Dyer

Audience Team Soho
Mischa Alexander, Erol Arguden, Brenton Arrendell, Farah Ashraf, Aiyana Bartlett, Ellie Bibby, Iona Brown, Auriella Campolina, Becca Carr, Geri Carr, Lanre Danmola, Anais Dos Santos, Bronya Doyle, Ben Falacci, Gabriel Harris, Oscar Holloway, Andrew Houghton, Hana Jennings, Lee King-Brown, Mariama Mansary, Tilly Marples, Faith Martin, India Martin, Kit Miles, Eve Millward, Benji Morris, Paul Murphy, Fiona Oakley, Jack Parry, Janisha Perera, Jesse Phillippi, Rosie Revan, Alexis Sakellaris, Genevieve Sabherwal, Genevieve Sinha, Johnie Spillane, Sami Sumaria, Dylan Sweet, Abby Timms, Lauren Tranter, Jade Warner-Clayton, Joanne Williams, Arthur Yang

Soho Theatre Bar
Abin Marson, Cazz Regan, MD Ridoy Khan, Lisa Gilroy, Sneha Adhikari, Anand Choudhary, Mike Giraldo Cifuentes, Sofia Dixon, Lauryn Giovanni, Bibin Gopi, Madeleine Hilton, Dizolele Isaac, Zara Mehrban, Tayafur Rahman, Fatemeh Sarebannejad, Anandhu Sudhakaran, Sian Walsh, Chi Whon Won, Zaza Wright

Soho Theatre Supporters

Principal Supporters

Dominic Webber Trust
Hedley and Fiona Goldberg
Michael and Isobel Holland
Linda Keenan
Soho Circle

Supporting Partners

Matthew Bunting
Stephen Garrett
Angela Hyde-Courtney
Phil & Jane Radcliff
Jonathan Rees

Corporate Sponsors

Adnams Southwold
Bargate Murray
Cameron Mackintosh
Character Seven
Financial Express
NBC Universal International Studios
Oberon Books Ltd
Soho Estates

Trusts & Foundations

The 29th May 1961 Charitable Trust
The Andor Charitable Trust
Bloomberg Philanthropies
Bruce Wake Charitable Trust
The Boris Karloff Charitable Foundation
The Boshier-Hinton Foundation
Chapman Charitable Trust
The Charlotte Bonham-Carter Charitable Trust
The D'Oyly Carte Charitable Trust
Dominic Webber Trust – Core Values
The Fenton Arts Trust
Fidelio Charitable Trust
Garrick Charitable Trust
The Goldsmiths' Company
Harold Hyam Wingate Foundation
Hyde Park Place Estate Charity
The Ian Mactaggart Trust
The Idlewild Trust
The John Thaw Foundation
John Lyon's Charity
KKL Charity
The Kobler Trust
Lara Atkin Charitable Foundation
The Leche Trust
The Mackintosh Foundation
Mohamed S. Farsi Foundation
#My Westminster Fund
Noel Coward Foundation
The Peggy Ramsay Foundation
The Rose Foundation
The Royal Victoria Hall Foundation
Santander Foundation
Schroder Charity Trust
The St James's Piccadilly Charity
Tallow Chandlers Benevolent Fund
The Teale Charitable Trust
The Thistle Trust
Unity Theatre Charitable Trust

Soho Theatre Performance Friends

Ali Braithwaite
Anna Bordon
Amanda Rajkumar
Helen Evans
Bhags Sharma
Rich Thorpe
Chris Thomas
Gary Wilder

Soho Theatre Playwright Friends

Maital Dar
Mrs Emily Fletcher
Liam Goddard
Andrew Lucas
Emma Whitting

Supported using public funding by
ARTS COUNCIL ENGLAND

The Virgins

Miriam Battye is a writer from Manchester. For theatre, credits include *Strategic Love Play* (Paines Plough/Soho Theatre), *Scenes with girls* (Royal Court) and *Find a Partner!* (NT Connections). For television, her credits include *Succession* (HBO), *Dead Ringers* (Amazon) and *Beef* (Netflix). For film, her credits include the upcoming *Extra Geography* for Film4/BFI/Screen Yorkshire.

by the same author from Faber

SCENES WITH GIRLS
STRATEGIC LOVE PLAY

MIRIAM BATTYE

The Virgins

faber

First published in 2025
by Faber and Faber Limited
The Bindery, 51 Hatton Garden
London, EC1N 8HN

Typeset by Brighton Gray
Printed and bound in the UK by CPI Group (Ltd), Croydon CR0 4YY

All rights reserved
© Miriam Battye, 2025

Miriam Battye is hereby identified as author
of this work in accordance with Section 77 of the
Copyright, Designs and Patents Act 1988

All rights whatsoever in this work, amateur or professional,
are strictly reserved. Applications for permission for any use
whatsoever including performance rights must be made in
advance, prior to any such proposed use,
to Independent Talent Group Limited,
40 Whitfield Street, London W1T 2RH

No performance may be given unless a licence
has first been obtained

A CIP record for this book
is available from the British Library

ISBN 978-0-571-40286-1

Printed and bound in the UK on FSC® certified paper in line with our continuing
commitment to ethical business practices, sustainability and the environment.
For further information see faber.co.uk/environmental-policy

Our authorised representative in the EU for product safety is
Easy Access System Europe, Mustamäe tee 50, 10621 Tallinn, Estonia
gpsr.requests@easproject.com

Acknowledgements

It's been a long road bringing this to an audience. Thank you Soho Theatre for championing it, and making it happen, particularly thank you to David, Eve and Max. Thank you everyone on team Soho. Thank you Faber, thank you Lily, Jodi, Dinah for helping me publish my final pink play.

Thank you to Ragevan, perhaps my favourite actor of all time. Thank you Zoë, Molly, Anushka, Ella and Alec. You are my dream cast, so respectful, curious, committed. And utterly gifted performers.

Thank you Rosie for your genius. Thank you Anna, Jodie, Roisin, Daze, Bethany, Raniah, Megan, Rute, Davin, Tricia, for all you've contributed. What a rehearsal room to be in. Thank you Polly for assembling our cast.

This play is personal, painful, something from deep within me. Thank you Jaz for making me feel proud and unashamed of what I've unearthed. You are a spectacular person and director, and have restored my faith in collaboration. Thank you for looking after my younger self and memories.

Thank you Alex Rusher, always, in everything. You make me able to do this job.

Thanks Mum and Dad. I love you.

The Virgins was first performed at Soho Theatre, London, on 29 January 2026, with the following cast:

Anya Zoë Armer
Mel Alec Boaden
Jess Ella Bruccoleri
Chloe Anushka Chakravarti
Phoebe Molly Hewitt-Richards
Joel Ragevan Vasan

Director Jaz Woodcock-Stewart
Set and Costume Designer Rosie Elnile
Lighting Designer Bethany Gupwell
Sound Designer Anna Clock
Casting Director Polly Jerrold
Intimacy Director Raniah Al-Sayed
Costume Supervisor Megan Rarity
Assistant Director Rute Costa
Production Manager Davin Patrick for The Production Family
Production Wellbeing Support Tricia Gannon for Artist Wellbeing Company
Production Assistant for Soho Theatre Daljinder Johal
Producer for Soho Theatre Eve Allin
Executive Producer David Luff
Company Stage Manager Roisin Symes
Deputy Stage Manager Jodie Jasmin Hicks
Assistant Stage Manager Daze Corder

For the virgins

Characters

Mel
twenty-two (male, not a virgin)

Joel
eighteen (male, virgin)

Chloe
sixteen (female, virgin)

Jess
sixteen (female, virgin)

Phoebe
sixteen (female, virgin)

Anya
seventeen (female, not a virgin)

THE VIRGINS

'I will always want it'
Alice Birch, *Revolt. She Said. Revolt Again.*

Notes

The play all takes place in the living room and bathroom of Chloe and Joel's house. Both rooms and the hallway between should be illuminated and visible at all times throughout the scenes.

The action in the bathroom is written in this font, and the action in the living room is written in this font, but the action happens simultaneously.

/ indicates overlapping dialogue

– is interruption

–. is a self-interruption

Words in [square brackets] are not said, or are indicated non-verbally

In future productions, the text can be adapted to suit different performance spaces.

This text went to print during rehearsals so may differ slightly from the text as performed.

A bathroom and a living room sit together, snug, separated by a hallway. The hallway passes between the two rooms and past the bathroom, on to the rest of the house.

A modest bathroom is illuminated in a bright, yellow light.

Chloe is brushing her teeth, looking in the mirror over the sink. She has a bit of Sudocrem on a spot. Jess is sitting on the side of the bath straightening her fringe. They are both sixteen, they are both in a combination of comfies and tights. They are very close friends. Politeness is out the window. Sometimes they can change the subject without alerting the other at all. Tinny music plays out Chloe's phone on the sink.

In the living room, a man (ageless, unusually confident), and Joel (eighteen, not) sit splayed on two armchairs, playing Super Smash Bros. on the Nintendo. Silence, concentration, just the sound of the occasional Falcon Punch.

Quiet. Just the music, the sound of teeth being brushed, of hair crackling between hot plates, and of the tapping of controllers.

This happens for about eight seconds.

Jess stops straightening her fringe. She looks at Chloe.

Jess Aren't you scared?

After a thoughtful moment, Chloe removes the brush from her mouth.

Chloe No. Are you?

Jess (*immediately*) No.

A stilted pause.

The sound of the tapping of controllers.

Chloe She's just a human, like, girl. I know she's in the year above but she doesn't bite. Despite what that graffiti says. – I mean I have heard from multiple sources that the graffiti is accurate. – But in those cases it was consensual. – But anywayanyway she won't. You don't bite friends.

Chloe starts brushing again.

Jess I meant about Tonight.

A brief pause.

going out

Chloe it's out out not just out

Jess all right are you not scared about that

Chloe stops brushing.

Chloe We have met boys before

Jess Not out out though

Chloe So

Jess Boys Out Out though

Chloe Boys aren't scary now

Jess No I know

Chloe They're just us in like trousers. Just us flattened out in like T-shirts and trousers

Jess Yeah –

Chloe They're as scared as us.

A beat. The end of that.
  Jess suddenly offers –

Jess I guess Joel's not scary

Chloe Oh my GOD my brother's not a boy

Jess (*unsure*) right, no.

Chloe Literally my brother ruins boys for everyone

Jess (*lying*) right, yeah.

Chloe JOEL CAN YOU PISS OFF INTO THE NIGHT OR SOMETHING –

Joel and Mel glance up for a beat. And back to the game.

Everything's fine Jess. We're not going to like get raped and die on our first night out to Lizard Lounge

Jess no I Know

Chloe We've been preparing for this for like one hundred years. We go in, pick one boy each to pull, do that pulling, then come home and eat the chicken dippers I've put in the fridge for us. At what part of that is dying occurring.

Jess It isn't. It sounded good.

Chloe Good.

Jess Good.

Chloe We're only pulling tonight. Maybe a bit of rub.

Jess Rub?

Chloe I don't know, don't make me say it again

Jess I don't want to rub

Chloe Pretend I didn't say it, just focus on the chicken dippers after

Jess We could just eat the chicken dippers now

Chloe No I'm really excited

Jess No I am too

Chloe It's literally the beginning Jess

Jess No I know I know that

Chloe It's literally happening. We're literally going to like grow old together

Jess I know I can't wait I can't wait

A bit of a pause.
  Jess suddenly shakes violently, stops.

Chloe Why did you just do that?

Jess thinks.

Jess I don't know. I think I just need to wee.

A pause. No one moves.

Mel wins the game, gives the smallest victorious exhale.

Lights fall.
  Lights up almost immediately.
  Jess is now brushing her teeth. Chloe is straightening her hair.

Mel is doing a solo level. Joel is standing, watching, bit bored.

Chloe We could do a whistle. If we're in danger.

Jess I can't whistle though.

Chloe Try though

Jess I know I can't though

Chloe Try though

Jess tries to whistle. Toothpaste goop flies out of her mouth.

fuck's sake Jess sorry I didn't mean that

Jess It's okay

Jess spits. She washes her toothbrush. Chloe watches her impatiently.

Chloe I mean *I* can do the whistle.

Jess What am I supposed to do though

Chloe I dunno.

Jess taps her brush on the side for a while.

Jess D'you not think people are gonna wanna rape me

A pause.

Chloe No I don't mean that. Sorry.

A bit of a pause.

We can think of something for you. Hand signals.

Jess What?

Chloe Hand signals. Like a sort of. Sign language. We can do it across the club if things get stressful.

Chloe sticks her hand in the air above her head and waggles it, demonstrably.

Jess What if it just looks like I'm dancing though

Chloe shrugs. Keeps waggling.

And aren't you more hot when you dance?

Chloe stops dancing. Thinks about this very seriously.

Chloe Yes actually

Jess So won't they want to have sex with us more?
If we're all hot hot hot dancing with our arms up
They're all just there for sex right?

Chloe Yeah.

Jess Yeah.

Chloe Men are visual creatures says Mum

A beat. Thinking.

Jess Unless our arms create. Like. Radius.

Chloe What?

Jess demonstrates dancing with lots of arms. Pushing away. She stops. Indicates –

Jess Radius.

Jess puts her arms away. Chloe looks at her for a long time.

Chloe No that's good actually. No that's good actually. That's not sexy at all.

Lights suddenly flicker off/on.
  Chloe is showing Jess how to dance. Stepping from foot to foot.

Jess I don't think that's the two-step.

Chloe Yeah it is.
One – two – steps.
One – two – steps.

Jess It's not called the 'two steps'
It's not just two steps

Chloe Yes it is

Jess I don't think it is Chlo

Joel leaves the living room and comes to the doorway to the bathroom.
  Chloe swings round to him immediately, protective of the space –

Chloe NO.

Joel Can you stop playing Raye so loud.

Chloe Lol you know the name.

Joel and Jess do everything in their power not to look at each other.

Joel (*not quite confidently enough*) Fuck off Haircut.

Chloe Fuck off. Haircut. Also.

Joel Fuck off I didn't.

Chloe Fuck off it DOESN'T WORK cos we both got them AT THE SAME TIME

Joel Fuck off BAD HAIRCUT

Chloe Fuck off boy who it takes FORTY MINUTES to trim your WEIRDLY NON HEAD

Joel Fuck you Chloe

Chloe Are you just HAVING CONVERSATIONS with Lisa do you just TALK TO our OLD-LADY HAIRDRESSER to have SOMEONE TO TALK YOUR DOG DOG FEELINGS TO

Joel FFFuck you Chloe

Chloe Fuck you Salad

Joel Don't call me Salad

Chloe Okay fine sorry Fuck you, Salad

Joel No one has called me Salad in about SIX YEARS

Mel pauses his game. Listens, a bit entertained.

Chloe Cos no one's talked to you in about six years, Sa-lad

Joel You're not funny.

Chloe You're SAh-lad You're not Ah-lad.

Joel You're not a l— you are one

Chloe Chicken Caesar Salad
EXTRA DRESSING

He looks from Chloe to Jess, panics a little, unable to counter, and fucks off back to the living room, where Mel does not greet him.
   Chloe looks back at Jess –

Chloe Am I abusing my brother if I call him Salad?

Jess What?

Chloe Cos he's like *visibly unhealthy* I mean

Jess No he's not?

   What!? Chloe looks at her, hard. A tense beat.

Chloe What?
   What does that mean? Why are you saying that?

Jess (*scared*) Nothing. Nothing.

   A weird pause.
   Joel suddenly runs back to the door –

Joel YOU'RE SHIT AND YOU'RE A VIRGIN AND YOU LIE

   He fucked it.

SORRY Jess

   Jess looks up, shocked to hear her name out of his mouth.
   Joel exits (to the rest of the house), furious with himself –

Jess

Chloe YOU'RE A VIRGIN.
   AND YOU'RE A BOY SO IT'S NOT EVEN OKAY!!

   Mel smirks. Starts playing a new level.

   Chloe turns back to Jess, chest heaving.

One day – this week – THIS WEEK I'm going to kill him. And eat him.
   I bet he tastes like fucking. Quorn.

Jess (*very small voice*) Lol I don't think you should talk about eating your brother

Chloe Why's he always getting all involved when my mates come round?

Jess makes a very small sound of discomfort. Lays her head on her knees. She's used to this.

He's always like coming down with his dishes, doing his dishes, then like drying his dishes, putting his dishes away, going up again, getting his glasses, coming down, doing his glasses, drying them, like holding them up and shining them like anyone cares about them shining, sitting in there all the time, on his phone like he's got anything to look at on there, standing in doorways, just being just *being* everywhere, constantly –

Joel has been moving down the hallway undetected listening to this, suddenly mounts the door with both hands – yells in –

Joel YOUR FRIEND'S HERE CAN YOU NOT GET IT ALSO FUCK YOU ALSO

He smacks the door frame and returns to the living room.

Chloe STOP BEING NEAR MY FRIENDS, FUCKHOLE

Music off. She rubs the Sudocrem off her face with a towel. Checking herself in mirror.

Joel picks up his controller, inflamed. Mel is smirking.

Joel Can I play Samus this time.

Mel doesn't answer. He taps his controller a few times.

Okay. Next time.

Jess Wait, do I need to look nicer when she comes in?

Chloe looks at Jess a bit too long.

Chloe No?

Chloe leaves.
Jess stands. She goes to her bag, gets her skirt out. She starts taking off her jogging bottoms.

Joel gets up.

Joel knocks on the bathroom door and comes in without a pause. Jess pulls up her jogging bottoms straight away.

Jess ohmygod

Joel goes straight to the sink without looking at Jess. He has no idea what to do so he fiddles with his toothbrush, picks it up.
He doesn't look at her. She looks at him in the mirror, then looks away.
He puts his toothbrush back. He runs a little water over his fingers. Wipes his hands with a towel.
He makes to leave. He stops by the door. He manages –

Joel Uhhm

He's already out of the door when he manages –

Howareyou?

He fucked it as he's already in the corridor.

Jess (*high*) Uh – good thanks you?

Joel yeah good thanks you? uhh

Terrible. He returns to the living room, miserably.
Jess, alone, finally breathes.
She is fine.
She suddenly dry-heaves in the toilet.
Chloe traipses back through the hallway to the bathroom, followed by Phoebe.
Phoebe is small and polished and worried about most things. She speaks very quickly.
She has all her bags and coat still on.

Phoebe – yeah I get it but what if someone like speaks sign language?

Chloe What?

Phoebe Like what if we're getting Harassed or whatever and we're signalling and someone starts like talking back to us?

Chloe I don't think that's gonna happen

Phoebe When Louise Zmitrowicz worked at Hotel Chocolat she was like waving her hands about and a deaf guy thought she was trying to talk to him.

They trudge into the bathroom.

Chloe Why was she waving her hands about
(*To Jess.*) – It's only Phoebe –

Jess visibly relaxes.

Phoebe I dunno it was Christmas and she's quite sort of. Hands. Isn't she

Jess Hi Phoebe

Jess moves a little towards Phoebe, who recoils instinctively.

D'you want to hug?

Phoebe Why?

Jess Because you've just arrived.

Phoebe Oh, okay then

They hug very briefly, then –

So apparently she was telling him More Pain More Pain in sign
  He complained and got a free H-box
  And she got suspended
  Cos she, like, Caused A Deaf Man Unnecessary Distress

Jess Oh right

Chloe What a wanker

Phoebe starts disrobing her scarf and coat. Jess starts taping her teeth with Sellotape.

(*From the mirror.*) Y'know *he* was probably just pretending to be deaf
  Get her to go really close his ear so he could y'know, Molest.
  You get all the pervs in Hotel Chocolat
  Cos they're all / too nice

Jess Too nice, mm

Chloe and the free samples

Mel (*not looking up from the controller*) you fucking anyone

Joel looks at him, surprised to hear his voice.
  A beat.

Joel no

Mel Well that's all right. That doesn't matter.

Phoebe She keeps hands in her pockets now. Ruined her life.
  – Remind me are we all pulling tonight?

Chloe Yeah

Phoebe wait why are we in the bathroom?

Phoebe's coat is off. She is holding it, dumbly. She turns to Chloe.

Chloe You can put your shit out there sorry I said your shit

Phoebe Okay

Chloe it's not shit –

Phoebe goes through her coat pockets during the next –

Phoebe I think the hand signals won't work –

Produces items that she puts by the sink: pressed powder, mascara, lip balm, keys, perfume, nail polish, rape alarm, drink spike bottle stopper, Maltesers, during –

I mean we could just play dead I heard when Taffy Prendergast got touched up in Pure she just slumped like a rag doll and they backed off but *actually,* someone else said you're supposed to make as much noise as possible, and look them in the eye so *they* know *you* know their identifiable characteristics but you're also not supposed to look at them at all, ever, because a look is an invitation –

Phoebe walks into the hall with her coat and goes into the living room by accident –

– so I really don't know how to do those both at once like am I looking at them and *not dead* or am I *not* looking and um –

She sees the boys. She halts, wide-eyed, terrified.

Dead.

Joel looks round at her.
  Phoebe stands very still.

A beat.

Chloe (*to Jess*) She's a bit not funny nowadays isn't she

Phoebe comes back into the bathroom. Still holding her coat. She stands there for a perplexed beat.

Phoebe Why is there a boy in your living room?

A beat.

Jess That's Joel. That's her brother. He's –
 (*Scared, off Chloe's look.*) He's not really a boy, is he

Phoebe No not Joel. Not *Joel*. Another one.

Chloe What? Another boy? No there's not.

Chloe goes into the living room.
Phoebe looks at Jess.

Phoebe I'm not prepared for this.

Chloe immediately walks out again and back into the bathroom.

Chloe There's a boy in my living room.

Lights fall.
Lights up.

The girls are standing at the back of the living room.
Joel very slowly turns his head to the look at the girls. He smiles in a mannered, terrified way.
He realises what they're staring at – Mel. Everyone is looking at Mel. Mel maintains his eyes on the game. He never looks back.

Lights fall.
Lights up.
In the bathroom, Chloe is pacing. Well, as much pacing as she can do in the tiny bathroom.

Mel is doing his wrist exercises. Joel watches, unsure how long this is going to take. He keeps glancing at the door, wondering if the girls will come back.

Jess His friend? I dunno

Chloe Joel doesn't have Friend

Phoebe Why's he called Mel

Chloe I don't know I don't name them

Jess Must be short for something

Phoebe Like Melon?

Chloe I don't know he's just called Mel can everyone stop screaming at me about it

During the next, Joel starts doing the wrist exercises too. A long moment of them doing it in unison until Mel realises and stops, and gameplay begins.

Phoebe Do you fancy him?

Chloe (*duh*) He's a boy?

Phoebe Yeah me too, good

Chloe Where did he come from

Jess Maybe he met him at the gym or something?

Phoebe Joel goes to the gym?

Jess (*off Chloe's look*) I – thought – he mentioned – deadlifting? No?

Chloe Why are you all of a sudden knowing things about my brother?

Phoebe That's so weird. I can't imagine Joel like. Picking anything up.

Jess He likes it apparently – (*off Chloe's look*) he hates it I don't know if he likes it or hates it

Phoebe Why's he going to the gym? Oh that makes me feel so sad. I'm just seeing a little Joel face on like a cartoon Hercules body – does he think the cartoon Hercules body will like distract from his –
   God you know I can't even think what his face looks like

Phoebe immediately exits the room, walks into the living room to look at Joel's face. Joel snaps round to greet her with a worried smile. Mel notices.

Chloe is still glaring at Jess.

Jess What?

Chloe Can you stop it?

Phoebe leaves the living room, returning to the bathroom.

Mel (eyes fixed on the screen) Why do you always look at them when they come in?

Joel looks at Mel, a little surprised to hear him speak.

Joel What?

Mel It won't help.

Phoebe Yeah he looks like an extra.

Jess What does an extra look like?

Phoebe Exactly.

Jess fake-laughs a little.

He like, doesn't have a face. He looks like a paper plate with a face drawn on it.

Chloe Can you all stop talking about my fucking fucking brother please?

They stare at her.

Phoebe Sorry.

Jess Sorry.

An uncomfortable pause.

Phoebe I'm gonna go look at the other one.

Phoebe rushes out to look at Mel. A bit of a pause.

Chloe When's Anya Goodrich coming?

Jess Why are you asking me that? You're the one who's been organising her.

Phoebe, satisfied, comes back in, listening curiously –

(*To Chloe.*) Did you just want to say it again that Anya Goodrich is coming?

Phoebe Wait who's coming?

Jess You just heard us say that Anya Goodrich is coming.

Chloe Anya Goodrich. Anya Goodrich is coming.

Phoebe smiles broadly.

Phoebe Wonderful.
Why?
How? I mean?
And why?

Jess Chloe invited / her.

Chloe I invited her.
She's like the whole reason we're getting in tonight.

Phoebe nods. She is suddenly very nervous.

Phoebe I mean great. Great. That's great. I mean she is in the year above. But no that's great. She's so pretty. It's great.

Chloe Yes it is. It's totally a non-event.

They all stand there silently processing.
Phoebe suddenly explodes.

Phoebe What if she doesn't get in because of us?
Oh my god. Please put me at the back in case I ruin it for everyone.

She sits on the side of the bath and starts putting on her coat again, panicked.

Chloe She's actually really sweet when you get to know her.

Jess When have you got to know her.

Chloe We talk. I really love her.

A beat.

Jess She's a bit stressful though

Chloe She's amazing

33

Jess She's not *actually* amazing like I know we're supposed to say she's amazing but she's not actually [amazing]

Chloe She's Anya Goodrich

Jess Yes I have heard of her

Phoebe you know she went out with Mr Paulson

Jess No she didn't

Chloe She did. She's the coolest hottest loudest girl in school

Jess Why's she coming here then?

Chloe That's very hurtful here is good

Phoebe suddenly stands up and addresses the room loudly, a finger aloft.

Phoebe Actually. We're FINE. We're gonna be FINE, actually.

Chloe and Jess look at her.

Jess What?

Phoebe smiles. She speaks delightedly, like this is the greatest power –

Phoebe We've got *boys*. We've got *boys here*. We show Anya Goodrich we've got boys here.

Phoebe suddenly exits into the hallway, finger still aloft and wearing her coat.

Phoebe edges into the living room and stands very quietly behind the boys with her back to the wall, trying to breathe quietly.

Jess (*a bit tentative*) D'you not think she's got a bit stressful though. Since she got, like, uh, molested
Is that the right word?
Uh
groped?

Chloe Isn't it SA now officially

Jess Is it?

Chloe I think so

Jess Don't things happen all the time on that road. Phoebe got flashed. And there's always that red van

Chloe That's just words though

Jess I even get stuff sometimes and I'm / rank

Chloe Can we definitely promise not to talk about this when she comes.

Jess She'll probs talk about it

Jess leaves the bathroom, goes to find Phoebe. Sees her –

Phoebe?

Joel turns round and jumps at the sight of Phoebe, now standing very close behind his chair.
Phoebe turns and scuttles into the hallway.

Phoebe The good one's deffo good enough for Anya right??

Phoebe leans against the wall in the hallway, gathering breath. Jess watches her warily.

Jess Are you all right?

Phoebe Okay good I'm fine then I think I'm just hungry.

Chloe yells out the door immediately.

Chloe DO YOU WANT TO EAT, PHOEBE?

Phoebe NO.
(*To Jess.*) I've done a test run and I know if I have three single vodka lemonades on no dinner I'll be fun and not vulnerable.

Jess Okay cool

Phoebe goes back into the bathroom, Jess follows.

Chloe What's going on with you.

Phoebe Nothing, just. Ever since I was a kid, I've been a bit, y'know. The look of men, y'know, big boots, big arms, picking up sacks of, like. Wheat.
Sometimes I get a bit –.

A beat. They are all looking at her.

I'm fine I'm absolutely – It's just a big night.

A beat.

Mel puts his hand into his pants and rubs suddenly quite aggressively, keeping his other hand on the controller. Stops. Joel pretends not to notice.

Chloe Sorry can I make a request?

Jess What?

Chloe When Anya Goodrich gets here can we all be a bit more normal and a bit less scared?

Lights fall.
  Lights up.

Anya is being shown the living room with Chloe. Anya is very beautiful and erratic and constantly looks like she is secretly laughing at you.

Chloe So, Anya, this is the living room
And these are boys

Anya Hi boys

Joel turns and looks at her, doesn't quite manage Hi.

Phoebe and Jess are standing in the bathroom, trying to subtly find the best position in which to look casual and cool and okay with themselves.

Chloe That's my brother, Anya, so don't [bother] about him. Sorry if he looks at you

Joel Fuck of Chloe

Chloe It's fuck off not fuck *of*

Joel FUCK – NOW

*He shoots a look at Anya, embarrassed.
Chloe leaves the room, thinking Anya will follow.*

Phoebe Let's just like laugh or something when she comes in so we look like fun girls

Chloe And here are the girlies –

*She goes into the bathroom and Jess and Phoebe animate. Phoebe starts laughing, loudly.
Chloe realises Anya isn't behind her.*

Oh. Where'd Anya go.

Chloe goes back into the living room.

Jess (*to Phoebe*) Lol she keeps saying her name.

Anya is sitting on the armrest of Joel's armchair. He is very, very uncomfortable.

Anya What does that do.

Joel indicates with his head at the screen.

Aaaaaaaoohhhhhh. You're really good at this.

Joel Okay.

Chloe Anya. Are you um. Coming?

Anya takes her time following Chloe out and into the bathroom; as she does –

Anya You're such a funny fuck, Joel. Honestly, do you know how much of a Funny Fuck you are

Unsure what else to say to Mel, Joel goes for –

Joel Fit.

Mel You think so?

Joel is startled he said the wrong thing. Mel eats some more crisps.

As Anya enters, Phoebe starts manically laughing again. Jess sits on the side of the bath again.

Anya Hi cheeky ladies.

Jess makes a face at this, thinks better of it.

Phoebe Oh my god heyyyyyyyyyyyy Anya!

Jess Hiiii.

Anya hugs Phoebe. Phoebe looks at Chloe and Jess over her shoulder as if she is being hugged by Dua Lipa.

Anya (*brightly*) Oh! You smell like orange juice.

Phoebe Oh!

They separate. Anya doesn't hug Jess.

Anya Lol we're in a bathroom. Are we drinking? When are we leaving?

Chloe Oh! We are we are we are

Chloe leaves quickly – for drinks –

Phoebe We're aiming to get there by ten-fifteen

Anya Oh that's too early.

Phoebe Okay sorry whatever you think

Mel suddenly puts down his controller. He starts rubbing his eyes. He gets into a really good rub, for ages and ages, so much so that Joel starts becoming a bit worried.

Anya (*looking around*) Midnight earliest – What's the deal with the boys then? Whose is whose?

A worried beat. No one looks at Anya.

They're both reallyreally fit.

A brief pause.

Jess I don't think they are.

A beat.

I don't think they reallyreally are.

Anya looks at Jess then, incredibly irritated.
  Chloe arrives with four glasses clutched in her hands and hands them to each member of the assembled group –

Chloe drinkiiiiiiiies

Chloe watches, worried, as Anya drinks. Anya grimaces.

Anya Oh. Did you put it with lemonade?

Chloe Oh. Um. Yeah.

Anya Okay bit weird but –

Chloe to Jess – 'why??' Disappointed, Anya drinks the whole lot in one go.
  The girls watch, worried.

Joel keeps looking at the door.

Mel What d'you keep looking at the door for?

Joel I need a. I need a piss

Mel No you don't.

Joel I, I do. I really do.

Mel All right. Well. Go and have a piss then.

Joel But they're –.

A beat.

Mel All right die then.

A beat.

Joel I could go in the sink in the –.

Mel actually stops playing.

Mel Why are you giving me all this *detail*?

Anya tongues round her mouth, unhappy. Chloe isn't sure what to do for a moment. Eyes Jess. Takes Anya's empty glass and begins to leave the room with it.

Anya Chlo how many rooms in this house?

Chloe Uh – it's a three-bed

Anya nods. Chloe leaves, unsure why she was asked that question –

At the same time, Joel gets up, exits to the rest of the house.

WHY ARE YOU IN THE HALLWAY
WHY ARE YOU IN THE HALLWAY
GET OUT OF THE HALLWAY QUICKER

Joel pretends to be cool and unaffected as they both hurriedly exit to the kitchen.

Anya So where's the other guy from

Phoebe We're currently unsure. Possible gym friend?

Anya Does Joel go to the gym fit

Phoebe I dunno, Jess said. She's known him since they were kids right

Jess Uh yeah sort of

Anya Oh my god *Jess. Twist.* Is something going on?

Phoebe gasps a very small amount.

Jess *No.* Something's not always going on

Anya (*bit stunned*) Okay . . . rude.
(*Very clearly to Phoebe.*) Are they coming out out

Phoebe I don't think so

Anya Ow. That seems a bit wasteful.

A beat. Anya pulls a wedgie out quite shamelessly. Surveying Jess.

Are you wearing that?

Jess What yes

Anya looks at her for a while.

Anya Okay, great. Okay. You can go at the back.

Jess smooths down her outfit, ashamed. Anya checks her phone.
  Chloe arrives with a 250ml bottle of vodka and a 1l bottle of lemonade. She crouches on the floor and mixes carefully. She tries not to use too much of the dwindling vodka.

Chloe what are we talking about

Anya Phoeb was just telling me about the boys

Phoebe to Jess – 'Phoeb!' Chloe is immediately worried. Anya snatches the glass as soon as it's poured –

Chloe What did she say?

Anya Allegedly they're not coming out with us

Chloe God no

Anya That's a shame. I mean I think Jess is a bit sad about that but

Chloe What?

Jess What?

Anya smiles in a pretend-coy way –

Anya Oh my god tetchy I'm kidding. I only know Frith and Fidge and Dan Waters and Bevan and Bevon and Pidge and

Doug Houghman and Jonesy and Jesus and Caplan and Jonjo and Shy Mike and the Tunnel lot and basically all the Year Thirteens from –

You are all aiming Year Thirteen right?

Nodding, lots of nodding. Jess a bit unsure.

Good thank god you don't want those groups of scaredy nons who just gawp at you

They can get fucking cumbersome

Nodding, 'yeah', 'cumbersome, yeah'.

Plus you can't evaluate quality properly when they're in a huddle

I can't sort of be doing with the virginal vibes tonight, I go older. Chloe you can probably go older

She notices Phoebe –

Sorry what are you doing? It's just in my eyeline and it's constant and it's really um distracting

Phoebe Oh I'm just making notes.

I tend to make notes.

A brief pause.

I can stop? I can stop.

She wordlessly puts her phone down.

Anya No you can make notes.

She waits for Phoebe to pick up her phone again.

What was I saying? Have I been talking for forty years actually? Why don't one of you guys talk?

The girls all look at Anya, frightened. No one says anything for a beat.

What's going on? Have any of you got any gossip?

A bit of a terrible pause. Chloe pretends to think. Phoebe looks at her phone for a beat.

Joel arrives in the living room again.

Joel I had to go outside

Mel Again with the detail

Joel Sorry, just that's why I took –

Mel Don't need the detail

Joel Right, sorry

Mel Bring it all down.

Mel holds out his hands like – bring it down. Joel, unsure, copies.

Phoebe Oh! Oh! Annika Sugarman got fingered over her tights behind a grave last week
 At her joint sixteenth. At the church hall. She was dressed as the Queen of Hearts. I think he was dressed as God

Anya (*not laughing*) That's funny. How d'you know that?

Chloe Oh Phoebe knows everything. Phoebe knows everything everyone's ever done.

Phoebe smiles, a bit proud.

She has an inventory.

Phoebe I don't know what it is, people just tell me stuff.

Anya You have a really, not-intimidating-at-all face, actually

Phoebe Thank you.

Chloe Plus she's been hiding in toilet cubicles at lunch since like, Year Seven

Phoebe Not. *Every* lunch

Anya laughs a little.

Jess She doesn't have a mum, though.

Everyone looks at Jess.

Sorry. Is that not okay to say?

Phoebe No. Yeah. I don't have a mum, so. I have to find out this stuff from somewhere

Anya Aw I'm sorry about that.

She pats Phoebe's knee. Phoebe nods bravely.

Phoebe Oh that's okay.
(*Rehearsed.*) I'm very lucky in very many ways.

A brief pause, a little awkward.

Sorry I hate it when dead mum gets brought in – always like. Sucks the air out.
Saysomethingelllllllse!

Chloe (*brightening*) She's got a story on everyone. Honestly.

Anya Really?

Jess Yeah it's amazing.

Anya Can I see it?

Anya holds out her hand to be handed the phone. Phoebe can't hand it over, protective.

Phoebe Uh

After a moment, Anya withdraws her hand. A weird moment.

Anya What's in there about me then?

A worried beat.

Phoebe Um.
The whole um. Molested? thing?
(*Hands to head.*) Oh my god is that word allowed. I'm sorry. I'm so sorry. Is that the official word.

Everyone looks down. Anya watches this for a moment.

Anya Oh. *Right.*

A beat. Anya smirks. Anya gets up and takes out her shiny make-up bag. Looks at herself in the mirror for a moment, deciding what to do. The girls, unseen by her, panic silently at each other.

Joel Shall we like invite them in?

Mel Why

Anya It's so funny.
Like everyone gets so fucking stressed about it. Honestly. I'm the one who's like sat there being normal and everyone else gets so embarrassing about it.
I'm not even.
Like four hundred thousand more interesting things have happened to me than –.

Anya picks up the pore vacuum from the side of the sink.

You shouldn't use this by the way. It damages your sebaceous glands or whatever the fuck

She puts it down with a thunk.

Mel They'll come eventually.
Why would we invite them.

Anya I'm starting to feel a bit weird about tonight. Um. Have you guys even been like Out before?

Phoebe We party. We've been to several parties.

Anya (*to Chloe*) Like what like birthday parties. Like have you even ever been out and done anything I'm not gonna have to like babysit you or something like I feel misled

Chloe suddenly explodes, without meaning to –

Chloe I've been Out. I've done stuff

Anya What? What have you done

A pause. Jess looks at Chloe, surprised.

Chloe Well. There was this boy in Gran Canaria.

Anya Oh my god twist dark horse exquisite

Chloe He um. We were outside the disco thing. And he put his hand. Um. He like. Grabbed on the uh, on my.
He grabbed my – like under my. Like grabbed, my Stomach. And um –

She demonstrates, hand outstretched, grabbing and holding a bit of lower body, hard.
A long moment of silence. Jess is staring at Chloe, concerned.

Anya Oh, right.

More silence.

That's not anything, though. That's not actually anything.

Chloe looks up at Anya.

Chloe Oh, is it not?

Anya How do you even grab a stomach?

A beat.

Chloe Right. Yeah. I don't, um. I don't know why I mentioned it.

Chloe glares at the floor, her face flushed. Jess is looking at her, worried. Anya exhales.

Anya 'kay. one sec

Anya, unimpressed, silently leaves the room. Chloe is bereft.

Jess You never told me about that?

Chloe What? Oh, I dunno.

Jess What did he do? With your stomach?

Chloe Oh it wasn't anything. It wasn't my stomach. It was –. It's not actually anything.

Anya stands outside the room, silently giggling to herself, not completely enjoying that she is, just shoulders bucking up and down.

Joel wins.

Joel Oh my god I won! I just won!

Mel Yeah. Well done

Joel slumps a little, feeling ashamed.

Joel oh sorry was that

Mel No don't shrink now what you shrinking for

Joel What?

Mel What you shrinking for

Anya goes back into the bathroom, all smiles and kindness.

I really like you, Joel. You're a cool guy. I'm really glad to be here with you. All right?

Joel Yeah?

Mel Yeah.

Mel looks back at the game. Picks up a controller. Joel looks back at the screen, baffled.

Anya Girls. I'm so sorry. I'm so sorry. Everything's just made loads of sense to me.

She bites her lip, a bit anxious about what she's about to say.

Can I ask you a potentially sensitive question.

A beat.

You're all virgins aren't you.

Lights fall.
Lights up.

Exactly the same position. Everyone is staring at Anya. A long pause.

Phoebe I mean *I* am.

A beat.

And *she* is.
And, *she* is.
So yeah. That's all of us. And that's all virgins.
So in answer to your question.
Yes.

A long pause.

Anya Well that's okay. That's actually so fine. That's so cool. Like I'm so glad I'm here suddenly. Like there's nothing to worry about at all.

A beat. The girls are unsure.

What's the plan then?

The girls stare at her, baffled. A long pause.

Jess Well. We were thinking there could be a whistle?

Lights fall.
  Lights up.
  The girls are in the same place but Anya is alight with a new energy.

Mel is standing, stretching. Joel is waiting.

Anya That's why it's really good to like work on your subconscious. Otherwise you. Like will always be / literally a virgin

Phoebe Scared? Oh

Anya Literally a virgin.

Chloe Oh right. Okay.

Anya Even when you're not literally a virgin.

Chloe Wowwww.

Anya It's like just like a small adjustment in your brain but honestly it'll make everything less stressful

Phoebe Okay that sounds

Chloe Less stressful

Anya (*genuine*) God you all look so freaked. It's making me sad.

Jess Um –

Anya Like there are two ways to deal with something mkay? You can try and prevent it from happening. Or you can change your mindset in relation to what is happening.

Jess Wait I don't understand

Anya That's annoying of you

Chloe Jess

Jess Like what are you talking about happening

Anya Losing your virginity Jess we're talking about losing your virginity sorry or do you want to drag it about forever

Jess stares at her, surprised at the venom.

Jess Are you? Is that what you're talking about or [the other thing]

Anya Or what?

Phoebe (*to Chloe, not really following*) Yeah to be fair I thought we were just kissing tonight?
(*Back to Anya.*) But, I'm fine with whatever. Whatever you think

She hiccups.

Anya Oh my god. I'm not telling you what to do with it. Or when to do with it. I'm only telling you what I wish someone had told me when I was on your side. Cos honestly I've found that the less of it I've had the better

Mel gently leaves the living room.

Jess (*small*) only that wasn't actually what the whistle's for um

Phoebe I have a question.

Anya Great. Love a question.

Mel pauses in the hallway, listening in to the bathroom.

Phoebe Sorry if this is wrong but. It's just. Um. Isn't like, like . . . promiscuity, sorry, I mean um um slutting it about, argh, no, just sex basically us just like going and having it isn't it supposed to be a sort of bad thing at this age? like isn't it a self-esteem thing? in girls? like there's none of it obv so . . . ? – or am I wrong or is that out of date? Sorry I didn't mean to speak.

Mel sits down, listening through the wall.

Anya That is quite out of date yeah
 Like sorry if this is disappointing or whatever but I got told it was this huge thing like bad or good but it's like neither. It's like

She puts her index finger in her mouth suddenly. And out.

Like that. Like a non-thing. And then you can start to be happy or whatever the fuck.

Phoebe (*another splurt*) Or there's the whole dad thing

Anya What?

Phoebe Sorry I didn't mean to speak again. But like if you haven't got a dad if he's left or whatever you look for like an alternative, um

Chloe Dad?

Phoebe No. No. Like a male figure to fill the. Gap. Uh – basically it's bad. No I've said it wrong. Um – one sec

She frantically searches through her phone notes. She stops, looks up.

I've got a dad so I'm fine.

Chloe (*putting a finger up*) me too

Jess Me too also

Anya You girls are so funny. You're literally so funny. You're so YOUNG.

Jess Um you're only in the year above –

Anya You're like girls from like the past or something – Phoebe?

Phoebe Yeah?

Anya Am I slutty to you?

Phoebe is stunned. Chloe gasps.

Do you think what I'm saying makes me slutty?

Phoebe gropes for an answer.

Joel comes into the hallway, spots Mel.

Joel What are you –

Mel puts a finger to his lips.

Mel You have to listen to women.

Joel frowns. But he stands and listens.

Phoebe No?

Chloe Phoebe don't be such a

Phoebe I'm sorry! I'm sorry for whatever I'm being!

Jess It's all right Phoebe

Anya Jess do *you* think that?

Jess What? No?

Anya You're sitting there doing a lot of stuff with your eyes is that what you think too?

Jess I don't think anything about you

Anya Stop looking at me [like that] then
(*To the others.*) Stand up.
Not Jess.

The girls stand; Jess is shocked –

She can watch. Since it doesn't *pertain* to her

Jess Chlo?

Chloe (*gently*) It's okay babe it doesn't pertain to you

Jess sits down. Anya sits on the toilet lid and waits for a moment to calm herself down.

Anya All right. Instead of us all getting stressed with each other and labelling each other sluts and rank unloved virgins or whatever how about we just stop all that and just focus on ourselves.

Phoebe D'you want us to close our eyes.

Anya No, that's a bit –.

Phoebe shakes her head, 'don't worry, sorry'.

Just. Y'know we're allowed to want shit now. Cos fine boys always want it they say but we, we are taught to think we don't.

Chloe thinks very hard. Phoebe's expression seems to retreat.

Do you want the truth girls. I think you maybe want the truth now

There's like this, beautiful, twist. We've been lied to, girls, like this whole time.

A beat.

You know when we were cavewomen, right, we used to moan and scream so everyone knew how much we wanted it.

Phoebe Oh my god, I heard that on a podcast.

Anya blinks at Phoebe, a bit annoyed she ruined the flow. Continues.

Anya Yeah. And then someone made us all shut up. But what if I don't want to shut up.

Chloe Ohhhhhhh.

Anya We've been like, miseducated, our whole lives to be afraid. But we're actually, quite powerful now. We're not in the awful past. It's not all like, God and Dad. It's us.

A beat.

It's about what we want now. Doesn't that make everything so much fucking better?

The girls don't understand. Anya is getting frustrated.

So what do you fucking fucking want girls?

A beat.
  Lights fall.
  Lights up.
  Anya is on the toilet. She finished weeing ages ago. She's just on her phone. The girls are in the hallway, waiting to be allowed back in. Jess is inflamed. The girls are trying to be hushed.

Mel is playing the game. Joel desperately wants to go back and listen. He keeps craning, trying to hear. Can't.

Chloe Where do you want it to happen?

Phoebe I dunno.

Jess I think we're being bullied.

Phoebe (*ignoring, not hearing?*) I've like literally never thought about it. There's been like a big red square over it

Chloe Me too or like fucking, drums?

Phoebe drums?

> *Joel intentionally loses the game. Oh no! Stands up, goes to listen.*

Chloe Like do you want to be lying down or do you want to be, like, picked up?

> *Joel immediately pivots hearing this, freaked, goes back to his seat. Mel titters. Joel starts playing again. But he truly cannot concentrate on anything with them in the corridor.*

Phoebe (*swallowing*) Picked up?

Chloe I dunno. Alita Bateman said her big boyfriend's always like picking her up and putting her against stuff

A beat.

I quite like that actually.
 Oh my god I've never said that before maybe I am like a dirty little ho

Phoebe Um am I allowed to say a normal flat bed or is that awful past of me

Chloe I think that's okay

Phoebe (*left field*) Do you have to make the sounds by the way?

Chloe What?

Phoebe Like porn sounds. They all do it. They do it in every category.

Chloe Did you watch every category.

Phoebe Just for research. They all do it.
They all.
'Uh.'

A beat.

Jess (*louder*) I think we're being bullied.

They both look at her. Anya heard it that time.

Chloe I don't think people get bullied any more Jess

Phoebe Um are you going to like, do it tonight?

Chloe I, dunno. I don't think we Have to but the point is we don't Not have to

Phoebe Right. So what am I not doing?

Chloe Whatever you want.

Phoebe (*confused*) I think I'm better with instructions than the opposite of um
Is is losing it or Not losing it the thing we're trying not to do any more

Chloe You make the instructions

Phoebe okay but what am I aiming for I just want to know what's good what's allowed what I'm aiming for

Chloe But

Phoebe That helps me

Chloe What do *you want*. That's what you're aiming for

Jess But that's not what Anya meant

Chloe Yes it is you just don't get it

Jess Don't pretend you got anything she said

Chloe I get that I feel better about tonight. I feel good about tonight, actually. Phoebe does too

Phoebe (*small*) I mean I still have a question –

Chloe That's what I get, Jess.

Jess Look. Phoebe. Being a virgin isn't even a thing any more. It's the opposite of a thing

Phoebe No it's not it's a massive thing

Chloe (*correcting, from Anya's theory*) No it's *not* actually a massive thing any more

Jess No it's – (*rerouting*) no yes it's *not* – exactly –

Chloe No – not like how *she* means it –

A battle for Phoebe's soul. Anya is listening now. She's a bit – moved or something? She feels like she's hearing her old self.

Jess No it's not massive we don't have to try and lose it

Chloe No it's *not massive* we can just let it go –

Phoebe It *is* a massive thing. It *is* a massive thing.

They look at her.

I can literally feel it

Jess No you can't it's too far inside

Phoebe No mine is so like loud isn't yours?

Jess Uh

Phoebe It's so heavy I feel like I'm wiping the floor with it

Chloe Don't say stuff like that –

Phoebe I'm surprised I can even walk with it

Chloe Don't say stuff like that when we go back in –

Anya is suddenly there at the door.

Anya Why, was it weird?

They jump, alarmed.

Jess It was quite weird but that's okay Phoeb

Joel, not being able to cope with focusing, suddenly stands, walks swiftly into the corridor –

Anya Lol why are you all standing in the corridor
I don't bite

Jess smirks.
   The girls start filing in apologetically; Phoebe is so confused –
   Joel – entirely missing them – arrives in the corridor saying –

Joel Would any of you like to share the common space – oh.

They're gone.

Joel re-enters the living room. Sits. Mel is entertained.

Phoebe I'm still a bit confused Anya

Chloe No you're not

Phoebe No I am going to say I am like a bit lost. Like I'm excited but I'm a bit lost.
What do I want?

Anya (*a bit impatient now*) You know what you want

Phoebe I don't

Anya Yeah you do. Under the fear et cetera. Shame et cetera. What's in that nice bit.

Phoebe thinks.

Mel 'common space'

Phoebe Can we start with what I *don't* want and go from there?

Chloe No Phoeb. We're not in the awful past. You have to know what you want or someone'll take it without you getting a say in it

Anya Chloe I literally love you so much

Chloe Oh

Anya turns to Phoebe.

Mel No it's not bad. You're like a

Joel scowls, waiting for more.

Anya How do you feel when a boy's in the room, Phoebe?

Phoebe What? Nothing, the same. Great. Really great.

Joel What
What am I

Phoebe is so confused and lost and scared now.

Anya Sure Phoebe? Doesn't the air go out of it a bit?

Phoebe (*brightly, giggling*) It's quite stressful when you say my name that much.

Jess Yeah. Can you chill a bit, Anya.

Anya What was that, *Jess*?

Anya glares at Jess. She's affronted.

Phoebe can everyone stop saying names atch

Joel What am I What am I

Jess Maybe we don't want boys every second

Anya I'm not talking to you actually?

Jess You don't have to want things all the time not everyone's a –.

She doesn't finish the sentence. She regrets speaking. Anya inflames.
Anya suddenly yells, eyes on Jess –

Anya JOEL?

The boys both snap round, shocked.

Jess (*light*) no don't

Chloe No –

Anya (*looking at Jess*) What happens when a boy's in the room Phoebe? What happens to your throat? Does it tighten up? Do you get very very stressed, Phoebe?

Phoebe (*confused as to what's happening*) No, I don't know, are you asking me or

Anya Are you sure you don't want anything – JOEL

Joel stands up, summoned.

Mel Don't what are you –

Chloe Anya . . .

Joel What do they want

Mel I dunno, but don't just go

Anya Maybe Jess should do it actually. She knows him best.

Jess No I don't. Do what? Also that would be Chloe

Chloe And I'm his sister so no. Also I don't know him. Also can we not

Anya FUCKING JOEL AT SOME POINT?

Joel goes, unable to not.

(*To Jess.*) You're such a little liar.

Jess stares at her, shocked. Joel dutifully enters. Chloe immediately drops down to the floor, covering her ears.

Joel What. Hi ladies.

Anya (*brightly, looking straight at Jess*) Okay Phoebe How do you feel now.

A pause. Jess is reddening. Phoebe is lost.

Phoebe What? Fine. I mean, I'm a bit stressed but it's separate to this it's not cos of.

Joel What am I doing?

Anya Just be yourself, Joel.

Joel What am I doing? Chlo?

Chloe don't call me Chlo

Anya Yeah don't talk for a sec, hun?

Joel looks down.

See this is what you're going to be faced with, Phoebe. You're going to have a boy opposite you. And you're going to have to know what to do about that.

Phoebe pauses.

Anya Just go up to him. Go on. Show him what you've got

Phoebe takes a step towards Joel. She suddenly erupts into laughter, runs backwards.

Phoebe No I can't do it!

Anya doesn't react. She holds up a hand to the others as if to say: 'Don't react. Don't rise to it.'
 Phoebe, sensing no support, goes back to her start position. She tries to stem her giggles. She gets in control of them. She looks at Joel. She takes a step towards him, still giggling.

Hh . . . hell—

She bursts into laughter.
 Phoebe crumples away. Joel tries to mask his embarrassment.

Anya Jess why don't you have a – ?

Jess *and* **Chloe** No.

A shocked beat. No one knows where to look.

Anya Oh my god. Okay.
 (*Indicating Phoebe and Jess.*) Joel pick one of them.

Chloe squeals – down on the floor into a ball now.
Joel is frozen, not wanting to pick Jess, not wanting to not pick her. Also wishing for death.

Joel Uhhh

He sort of moves, oddly, nowhere.

Anya Pick one and go to her like you're at the club or whatever the fuck tonight
Go on. Show her what you've got

A pause.
Joel makes a random, badly articulated step forward towards no one in particular and Phoebe SCREAMS, giggling and stressed and flattens herself frontwards against the wall and Jess, not knowing what to do, copies, but unable to make a sound.
A stressed beat. Joel is humiliated. A silence descends.

Anya All right Joel babe you can go thankyou

He scuttles out, not before never being able to un-hear –

We need to try with someone real

He makes a little noise then and –

– moves into and sits in the living room in private hell.
Mel stares at him, a bit alarmed.

Sorry about that Chlo.

Chloe slowly stands up.

Chloe That's okay Any

Jess sits down on the bath.

A beat.

Joel Why does every single person in the world think I'm like a barnyard animal.

Mel looks at Joel.

Anya (*to Phoebe and Chloe*) I just.
I want this to be normal for you.
I have this sudden massive urge to help you girls.

A beat. Phoebe has never been more terrified. Chloe has never been more enlivened.

Mel It's all right. That goes away.

Anya It won't always be like this. I promise.

Lights fall.
Lights up.
Quiet. The girls are practising brushing their tongues. Light, gentle. It's a little strange, unexplained. Anya seems to be guiding. Relaxed. Jess is sitting out of this activity, still sitting on the side of the bath, increasingly upset and uncomfortable. Occasionally, Phoebe or Chloe have to take a break. Jess may occasionally leave the room, trying to find somewhere else to be.

Joel is sharing energetically. Mel is eating an apple, diffident.

Joel and that's the thing like I think I've missed it. And now it's like really hard cos it's like. Well. The whole. You need customer service experience to get the job but you need a customer service job to get the experience Sorry is it okay that I'm saying all this to you?

Anya It's not even that far off this to be honest

Mel nods at him. A beat.

Joel Right good cos like I don't even –

Mel Do you even want girls?

Joel (*startled*) What? Yeah?

A beat.

Mel I don't mean do you want boys.

A beat. He realises Joel is looking at him, absolutely rapt.

What I mean is. Do you even want girls right now. Like you seem like a guy with stuff to figure out. You're always really quiet at the weights. You're so [focused]. I assumed you were probably thinking something interesting

Joel Really

Mel Yeah I dunno

Joel I mean I think about stuff

Mel Yeah

Joel Some of that stuff is girls

Mel Okay

Jess walks into the corridor. Feeling panicked that her friends are slipping away.

Joel Like I want. I would, quite want some girls right now. I mean a girl. Now. I don't want all of them, I'm not a. One of those um. Like one of *those*. I only want One once. Forever. uh

Mel D'you want a specific one? Is there one you want?

Joel (*a lie*) No?

A pause.

Mel No?

Joel No.

A beat.

Mel mm. Then I think you're doing too much.

Anya And then it's just a little bit back from that.

She goes a little further back. After a moment, slightly gags. Phoebe and Chloe follow. Both gag.

Everyone tries again, at varying levels. This should not be horrifying. Everyone is being gentle with themselves and their limits.

Mel (*relaxed*) I wish I could take it off you, you know. Like. Just fuck that off. You'll feel better when it's gone

Phoebe coughs, a bit of a coughing fit, an objection to the brush in her mouth. Has to stop.
The coughing continues for a while. Everyone looks at her.

Anya It's all right. Don't worry.

Joel I'll never. I've missed it.

Mel No. Don't with that.

Joel I have

Anya That goes away. Eventually it goes away.

Mel Mate. Mate. Mate.
You have like no idea what's going on do you.

Joel looks at him. A question.

Jess goes to get another drink.

Mel They approach now. *They* do.
You just have to let them.
Otherwise it's honestly not worth the ag.
Otherwise, you just go home, honestly.
Otherwise you just take yourself home, honestly.
And that's fine. Get a good night's sleep. Work on yourself. Try again next time.

A beat. Mel chews for a little bit longer.

But *don't* try. That's the thing.
You don't do the trying.
You don't do the approaching.
You don't even look at them.

You don't even look at any one of them one time the whole night. Honestly.

It's like a magical spell you do without doing anything.

You dress yourself well and you smell good and you don't get too fucked up so you're sloppy but you don't look at them. You honestly just look over their heads. Talk to your mates. Enjoy the music. Enjoy yourself. Did you know you can *enjoy* yourself? Dance a bit if you want. Did you know we can dance now. If you're worried, just keep it to the side-to-side step but honestly don't even worry about it.

A beat.

You don't even have to *do anything*. *Don't do* anything. If you *do anything* you get in trouble anyway.

He puts his hands up, 'look, no hands'.
He laughs.

Let them.

Joel takes in Mel's hands. A beat.

Joel But. What do I say.

Mel Nothing.

Mel brings his hands down. Keeps eating.

Joel I'm confused.

Mel Well don't say that. Don't ever say that.

Joel Okay.

A moment of confused silence as Mel finishes the entire apple.

Mel Do less. Like. Behave naturally.

Joel nods, thinking carefully about this idea. Mel stands, looking for somewhere to deposit his apple core.

Joel Really?

Mel Really.

Joel takes this in, nodding.

Mel suddenly breezes through with his apple core; the girls freeze. He drops it in the pedal bin. He returns to the living room, passing Jess on the way.
The briefest moment in the hallway –

Mel Y'all right

She looks behind herself expecting someone else there.

Jess no

And Mel's back in the living room.

The girls watch the space where he was.

Mel It's so good now. This dayandage. It's so beautiful. You can just be yourself.

A beat.

I think the past was like so much more stressful for us

Lights change to a striking pink.
The girls rise from their seated position. Just Jess remains seated. Anya leads the girls like the Pied Piper out of the bathroom and into the hallway –
Lights up.
Anya is teaching the girls how to dance. They copy exactly.
It appears to be very simple, but it is meticulous. It's not overtly sexy. This is not a TikTok dance. This is simply how to make your body into a shape that won't embarrass you. That will make you look good.

Mel is offering up clothes to swap with Joel, whilst still playing the game. Joel is enjoying trying them on. Seeing how they fit, moving about a bit.

Jess remains in the bathroom, still seated, and alone. Her body the shape of an objection.

Phoebe I need a wee!

She leaves the hallway. Legs a little wayward as she moves, she finds Jess, immediately slumps –

I'm so unspecial out there, I'm like, a member of the wall

Phoebe puts her forehead against the wall, perhaps.

Why are you in here?

Jess I'm objecting. I'm a conscious objector.

Jess sinks into her knees.

Phoebe Is it going to be too much for me? Like a body, that close up to me?
 I find hugs hard.

A beat.
  She suddenly gulps quite a lot of her drink.
  Anya realises Phoebe's gone –

Anya Oh thank GOD let's go in now they're not [with us].

Chloe What? But –

Anya Come on let's get the fit one

Chloe What? What are we doing with him?

Anya's immediately into the living room. Chloe, unsure, following, collecting Anya's drink.

The duo arrive inside the living room. Joel returns to his seat, absolutely ignoring them.
 Mel notes this, a bit proud.
 Anya is a little baffled by the cool reception.

Phoebe Can I –

Phoebe takes Jess's immediately offered drink. Deposits it into her own glass. Drinks.

Anya elegantly places herself on the arm of Mel's chair.

Anya Um. Can we watch?

No response.
  More playing.
  Chloe doesn't know where to go, or what to do.

Jess Do you feel better about tonight?

A bit of a pause as Phoebe thinks about this.

Phoebe D'you think one day you'll stand in front of a boy and just be standing there and not. Well not doing anything at all just be standing there.

Jess I don't know

Chloe (*pretending*) I'm ssooo drunk.

No response. Chloe exits –

Phoebe decides to leave as Chloe swings into the bathroom –

Chloe I'm ssooo drunk.

Jess No you're not.

Chloe (*dropping the drunk act*) Can you stop ruining everything?

Phoebe How are you, Chloe? Sorry, I mean, how scared are you?

Chloe Um . . . I'm kind of not any more. This is becoming normal.

Phoebe passes her into the living room, thoughtful.

She watches the boys from the back wall. Trying to stand and feel better. Drinking steadily.

Are you coming in yet?

Anya starts trying to play-fight with Mel occasionally. Nick his controller. Cover his eyes. He's nice about it, but not playful.

I can't hold everything together in there and out here. JOEL'S in there and what if he SPEAKS to her what if he makes her SAD

Jess I'm getting so like. I'm getting so like. What if she's dragging us down with her

Chloe She's dragging me up

Jess Let's not do anything tonight. Let's just stay home and not do anything.

Chloe That's completely a fucking insane thing to say

Jess It's not

Chloe We just get through tonight. And then we just be like *actual girls*. Not *virgin girls*. We don't drag it round any more. We drag round something else.

A beat.

Jess D'you remember before? I liked everything before.

Chloe No you didn't

Jess I did I liked it when we were allowed to not want stuff

A beat.

I wish we could just do it to each other. I wish that counted.

Chloe Don't say stuff like that.

Jess No I didn't mean like

Chloe Don't say stuff like that if she comes back –

Jess I don't care if she comes back I only care about you coming back.

A pause.

I just meant like –

Jess puts her hooked finger in her mouth.

– that. Imagine if that was it.

> *Chloe looks at her. A beat. Jess takes her finger out, sheepish. A little laugh.*
> *Suddenly, unexpectedly, puts her hooked finger in Jess's mouth.*

Chloe Done!

> *Jess laughs, puts her hooked finger in Chloe's.*

Jess Done!

> *They laugh, fingers in mouths. Stay like this for a moment. Laughing, stopping laughing, laughing again. Finding it oddly comfortable.*

> Mel suddenly wrenches the controller off Anya and she falls off her place on the side of the chair. It's pretty terrible. Phoebe looks at the wall.
> No one keeps playing the game.
> Anya stays on the floor for a moment in shame. Then stands up. Exits, flicking hair.

> *In the hallway Anya almost buckles in embarrassment but maintains herself all the way into the –*
> *Bathroom. Chloe pulls her finger out immediately. A beat.*

Anya Is this house like a mad place

> *She turns and goes, perplexed.*

Mel what I didn't do anything

> *Chloe pulls Jess's finger out of her mouth. They sit there in slightly ashamed silence.*
> *Anya stays in the hallway. Back turned. She does some slightly unusual, subtle movements. Hands on hips. Shoulders. Trying to. To place. Place herself. Herself on. On the ground.*

Phoebe (*barely heard*) oh my god I'm the only one in here

She turns to the wall, perhaps.

Jess I don't think I have proper Want, Chlo. Any actual, proper, inside me, low, bottom, inside me, circle-circular, under-skin, humming, tiny-little, um loud, in me,
Want
I don't.
I don't want anything or anyone.

A pause.

Chloe You do, Jess. You want things.

Jess (*scared*) I don't

They look at each other then. It's very hard for Chloe to even let this truth into the room.

Stop lying I know you do.

A moment where they really look at each other.
Chloe suddenly stands up. Wipes her finger on her tights and goes.
Jess stands. Thinks about that thing she's not allowed to want that she wants.
Anya decides to go into the living room.

Anya Can we get some fucking fucking music on please

Chloe goes into living room.
Mel's outta there.

Mel goes into the bathroom.
Jess immediately wants to get out. Mel does a chivalrous gesture as she passes.
Joel goes into the corridor.
Jess and Joel in perfect synchronicity arrive in the hallway at exactly the same time.
They look at each other for a long moment.

During the next, Phoebe and Chloe help Anya pick music. It's fun.

Throughout the next, Mel gently digs through the girls' make-up bags, curious.
In the middle –

Joel Jess –.

Jess Hi.

Nothing more. He stops himself like he's already fucked up. Shakes his head a little. Looks up at the ceiling.
But. He recoils, instinctively.
They look at each other, quietly afraid. Her hand retracts.
Mel looks his head out the door, sees what's happening, immediately retreats. Leave them to it. Hands up. Don't do too much, mate, he thinks. He's hopeful, actually.
Jess takes one step towards Joel, unsure. A polite invitation. He has no idea what he's supposed to do. So does nothing.
Confused, she takes another step. Hopeful. He remains still.

Jess I thought you.

She is hoarse with desire and fear.
Another step. The very furthest she is able to go.

I thought you wanted this.

He does, Jess! Oh, he does! He, panicked, raises his hands above his head. 'Look, no hands.' He thinks he should probably do that. Hoping she'll come closer.

Joel (*tiny, helpless*) I don't know what I'm supposed to do!

She recoils, not sure what he is saying, just knowing he is humiliating her.
She steadies herself. Turns away.
He disappears into the bathroom to breathe –
Either side of the wall, they are both quietly hurt.
In the bathroom, Mel notices Joel, and jumps.

Mel What? What happened?

Joel literally has no idea what's happened. Mel helps him sit on the closed toilet seat, calms him. He's shaking.

Joel I did what you said – I didn't do what you said don't do

Jess (*to herself*) stop eating asap

Joel What did I do wrong?

Joel is looking at Mel like he has all the answers, like he will save him from this fate. It fills Mel up in a rare way. He cradles this boy.

In the living room, Anya taps her empty glass, indicating to Chloe.
   Chloe takes her glass off her, irritated, and stands up to exit.

Jess Chlo?

Chloe One sec

She goes off. Jess sags.

In the living room, Phoebe and Anya are listening to music.

Phoebe I have a question

Anya Great. Love a question

Phoebe What's sex like after you've started doing it

A pause.

Anya It's not even that bad

Phoebe looks at her then. Disappointed.

I don't even mind it

Phoebe oh.

Chloe returns with the bottle.

Jess Chlo am I not a *bit* good-looking?

Chloe (*totally blindsided*) What?

Chloe halts.

Jess Just tell me. Am I not. It's better if I know now.

Chloe I don't think I'm the one who's supposed to answer that.

A pause.

Jess Oh. Okay.

A pause.

Chloe *I* think you're beautiful.

A brief pause.

Jess why did that make me feel bad

Jess sags. Chloe watches her, unsure what to do.

Mel You're so close mate. You're not far off at all

Mel smacks Joel on the back. Brings him to standing. Speaks low, conspiratorial, a gift –

you know they're not that good

To Chloe's surprise, Jess gets herself up. Chloe watches as she goes into the living room.

The girls look up. Chloe follows Jess, peers in.

they don't solve it all. so keep calm

Jess looks at them all.

Jess What's next then. What happens next. Anya?

Anya looks up last.

Lights suddenly fall.
  Lights change.
  A brief moment –

In the living room, the girls prepare their apparatus to get fucked up with.

In the bathroom, the boys put pomade in their hair. It is tender, the way Mel shows Joel how to do it well.
  Lights to full.

Behind, the girls are precisely passing round and sniffing nail polish in a bag. This is the absolutely precious, diligent labour of fucking oneself up.
  The choreography of the bag should always go in the right order and should be dynamic and throughout the dialogue. Just Anya remains lain on the floor the whole time.

Jess (*quiet*) is anything happening yet

Phoebe This is mad

Chloe (*quiet*) has anyone else been called a whore since they were like six years old cos I have and I still have no idea what it means! still!

Jess is anyone else feeling different
  to now to before, or just nothing

Joel (*the pomade*) Is it okay

Mel yeah it's really good quality actually

Chloe (*quiet, giggly*) Like what did I do?
  Like did I do something or is something you can just read on my face?

Jess This doesn't do anything

Chloe Shut up it does

Jess But it's just nail polish

Chloe Well we're out of alcohol

Jess Am I doing it wrong

Chloe Yes

Phoebe It makes me feel red anyone else

Jess huffs harder.

Chloe (*not quiet enough*) I've always assumed I'm going to be a whore??
 That I'm going to be really randy for sex or whatever I've never used the word randy before haha

Phoebe Can I ask a question

Jess When are we going out

Phoebe Oh my god remember that remember the out going

Chloe chicken dippers

Phoebe the out out going

Chloe (*on behalf of Anya*) it's too early

Jess okay but can we not wait too long
 Can we not wait too long
 Cos it'll be too late

Phoebe what's happened to Jess

Jess else I'll miss my window can we go now

Phoebe Can I ask a question

Mel Not too much not so much that you can see it

Chloe Can I lose someone else's virginity? Like for someone else?

Jess What?

Phoebe suddenly gets herself off the floor, goes, ignored –

Phoebe goes into the bathroom.
 She silently stands herself in front of the boys. It is a moment of true selfhood. Hands raised. She stands there. The boys find themselves, eventually, rapt by her.

Chloe Like can I put it on a piece of paper like VIRGINITY and rip it up. No one can tell anyway

Anya (*from the floor*) You can tell.

Everyone looks at Anya. A beat. Then –

Chloe Is there another way to lose it?

Jess What?

Chloe I dunno obviously not but is there

Jess Whose would you lose for them

Anya YOU

Anya laughs.

Jess What?

Anya need it could do with it I mean

A beat.

lighten her up

Jess is a bit offended.

Jess lighten me up?

Anya just waggles her hand from the floor as though that's supposed to make sense.

Chloe You are quite a heavy person in general actually Like a bag or something.

Jess What?

Chloe A plastic bag with a big bit of dough in it

Jess What?

Chloe I dunno

Jess Why am I plastic bag with a bit of dough in it.

Chloe I dunno I dunno why I said it

Jess Do you agree Phoebe?
  Where's Phoebe?

Anya Are there any like small small snackettes.

Jess Why am I a plastic bag with dough in it?

Chloe I don't know.

Jess Why am I a plastic bag with dough in it

Chloe I don't know sorry

Jess is furious. Sulks.

Anya just something to put in my mouth.

Eventually Phoebe realises she feels entirely un-rapt by them.
  She brings her hands down.

Phoebe Thank you. This was very unformative.

That unformative experience leads her back to the living room.

Anya looks around.

Anya has everyone died whilst still sitting up

Phoebe (*returning, standing*) Can I ask a question?
  What if you drag it around forever. Like what if you do what happens. What actually happens.

She sits down, pleased. Everyone is looking at her.

Like what if I just don't.
  Like I've done some research and what if I don't.
  I don't actually think it has a biological disadvantage. Oh it was more of a comment than a question.

She suddenly lies down, a bit zizzed, and pleased. No one really knows what to make of that.

Anya (*after a moment*) She will do it

Jess Shut up that was nice

Anya It was a lie

Phoebe (*small*) no it wasn't

Anya she'll be on her back within six months guarantee

Jess You can't SAY that

Anya lifts her head up to look at Jess, inflamed.

Anya yes I can. I can say ANYTHING about this

Jess No you can't

Anya yes I can watch me

Chloe Jess

Anya I can literally say ANYTHING about this and it's right

Jess No you *can't*

A beat. Anya sits up – right on at Jess now. Jess is astonished by Anya's power.

Anya Would you LIKE TO TELL ME THAT I AM WRONG JESS WOULD YOU LIKE TO TELL ME THAT I AM WRONG ABOUT THIS SUBJECT MATTER
 WOULD YOU
 WOULD YOU REALLY

They heard that. Pause for a moment.

Jess is simply overpowered by this. She would not.

Everything I say is ALLOWED
Because of what happened.

A beat.

Everything I say
 It's *because of what happened*
 Nothing I say
 Isn't *because of what happened*

>Nothing I *do*
>No ideas or thoughts or the fact that I'm a vegetarian my move towards wearing more colour
>>Isn't *because of what happened*
>>Even if it isn't that
>>*Even* if I just *do*
>>*Because I want to*
>>It is all because of what happened
>>*Apparently*
>>SO I'M ALLOWED.
>>Because of WHAT HAPPENED
>
>*She's really saying this to Jess.*

Jess Okay

Anya GOOD.

Phoebe good

Anya (*pointing*) Yes. Yes. I've decided it's GOOD, actually.
 I'm so SORRY I've decided I want something to be GOOD JESS
>That I can make some FORTUNATE, actually, JESS COS
>I can do whatever THE HELL I want.
>AND NO ONE EVEN EVER NO ONE
>No one
>Not one of you no one –.

Anya is very still for a moment. She is not emotional. She suddenly shuffles up closer to Jess. It's a bit of surprise. Right next to her. Like she really wants Jess to hear this.

It's not even a big deal

>*A beat.*

It's just what will happen the more attractive I get Mum says
>People want to have sex with you when you're attractive so

So like.
At least I'm not not attractive.

She smiles, sort of. A very unhappy smile.

[don't] tell me I'm wrong

A pause.

Jess But it's not because of that though

Anya looks at her. For the first time she seems genuinely, brightly surprised.

Anya What?

Jess What happened didn't happen because of that though

A bit of a weird pause.

Anya Are you saying it didn't happen because I was attractive?

Jess No I'm saying, what happened – wasn't sex

A beat. Anya doesn't understand – can't – won't – can't –

Anya So why did it happen then?

Chloe Jess just

Anya No absolutely stop talking why did it happen then?

A beat.

Jess I don't know. I'm really sorry

Anya Why don't you know though if you're saying things

Chloe What's everyone talking about

Jess I don't know why it happened

Anya FUCK you RIGHT NOW

Joel hears this and goes to listen in the hallway. Mel follows – surprised Joel is taking the lead.

Jess I'm sorry

Anya Are you just speaking? Why are you speaking?

Jess No I didn't mean anything. I'm really sorry I spoke, I thought –.

Anya Are you saying loud things about me Jess. Are you saying things about me Jess. Are you saying things about me Jess are you Jess.

Jess No

Anya DON'T EVEN LOOK AT ME AGAIN

Jess I'm sorry. I'm sorry. I don't know why it happened it's not your fault it's not because of you at all

Anya WHY THEN

Phoebe (*unheard*) it's them

Anya WHY THEN

Jess It's not to do with us or want or any of it

A beat.

Anya Jess wants Joel and I'm the big slut

Chloe Don't say it!!

Jess No!!

A beat.

Anya She wants him, she like bad hard et cetera wants him

Chloe No!

Anya The high priestess wants to be bent over the back of a chair like the rest of us

Jess Stop it!

Joel doesn't know what to do. He goes into the bathroom. He reacts privately to what he's heard. At some point returns to the hallway.

Phoebe puts a finger in the air.

Phoebe Idon't

Anya (*off Chloe's look*) Oh don't worry, Chlo babe. Remember the 'they want us' rule doesn't *pertain* to her Yeah that doesn't *pertain* to Jessica Surname

Jess Why do you hate me?

Anya (*very loud and very with a question mark*) I DON'T KNOW?

Phoebe IlikeJess

Anya You're not good, Jess. I know your thing is that you sometimes just say like your *one thing* just open your head and *say whatever one small shit comes out of it* and everyone fucking like *loves you for it*, but honestly if I'm honest if I'm totally honest it's only like a five per cent success rate.

Jess Literally same. Same. You're just a loud person.

Anya Call me when someone has enjoyed your company ever.

Jess Fucking! Same! Exactly the same! The same!

A brief pause. Anya suddenly storms out of the room.

The boys scarper – Joel offstage – Mel into the bathroom. Anya left.

Anya (*almost unheard*) where are they fucking GOING GOD

She makes a truly infuriated noise. Trying to calm down, she opens her bag looking for her gum and drops everything on the floor. Everything is spilled out. She's trying to locate and them open the gum packet during the next. She's frustrated to see her hands are shaking a bit.

Jess She's a shit person

Chloe Don't *say* that. She's my friend and now you're making us have secrets

Jess She's not your friend.

Chloe Shut *up*, Jess.

Jess Why are you trying so hard.
　I liked you before this. I like you now. Why are you pretending to be a completely different person.

Chloe Fuck off says you.

Jess Fuck off.

Phoebe Fuckoff

Chloe Fuck off says you though. You're like the least secure person I've ever met

Jess Stop using the word *secure* all the time like it actually *means* something

Chloe It *does* mean something it's not my fault you don't know words

Jess No you heard it ONCE and you pretended you knew what it meant like MOST of your fucking life
　Stop it
　Stop being a pretend you

Chloe What's the other thing I'm supposed to be then? Myyyyy totalself?
　I wish you wouldn't be your total / self
　No one likes you at all except me I am your literal only whole social life SINCE WE WERE SEVEN

Jess Fuck off fuck off fuckofffuckofffuckoffffff

Phoebe I like Jess

Jess You're the fucking notactuallysecure one

Chloe That wasn't even a secure FUCKING sentence

Jess Is there even any part of you that's you now you're like a human fucking version of a fret do you actually just walk through life with your fingers crossed??????????

Chloe stares at her, perplexed.
She suddenly stands up.
She jumps up and down a bit, frustrated kid. Stops. Hands.

Chloe MAKE

.

SENSE

.

ONCE.

Chloe leaves, blood pumping. Sees –
Anya on the floor, distressed. She's got crap on her hands. A beat.

Chloe Sorry about her

Anya This always happens, you know

Chloe What?

Anya When you start going out. At some point someone's got to decide how to deal with – like the other girl.
The problems start
When you've got someone who's not in the bracket

A beat. She finds her gum.

Honestly you'll start feeling like you're going clubbing with her on your back
Just. Shed.

A beat. Chloe doesn't know what to do. Jess heard every word.

You'll honestly feel so much better

A beat. Chloe is processing. Trying to decide what's next. Suddenly –

Chloe (*urgent*) Is he in there?

Anya looks at her then.

Anya What?

Chloe The boy the boy is the boy in there

Anya Yeah . . .

A beat. Anya is fully regenerated into the cool girl again. She is smiling at Chloe.

Oh my god twist.
D'you wanna go in there

Chloe I dunno. Yes.

A beat.

Is that all right is that allowed.

Anya Of course. Of course it is.

Anya stands back. Arms up.

Like. Be my guest.

Chloe goes closer to the door.

Chloe What do you do in there

Anya Whatever you want
Such a dark horse

*Anya blows a kiss, off she goes.
A moment of quiet.
Chloe goes closer to the door.
In the hallway, Joel returns. He sees Chloe standing outside the door.*

Joel What are you doing

Chloe Nothing. Go away.

Joel He's in there.

A beat.

Don't go in there

Chloe Stop looking at me.

Joel *Chloe.*

She says nothing.

Look I'm not going to tell you what to do

Chloe good cos that would embarrass everyone

Joel But you don't have to –

Chloe Fuck *of*

He very gently laughs at that. Continues.

Joel You don't have to go in there

Chloe Don't look at me like TURN AROUND I don't want you like watching while I go in there

She doesn't. She can't.

TURN AROUND. TURN AROUND.

Joel takes a step towards his sister.

Joel Chlo.

She doesn't move.

Chlo.

She turns to him –

Chloe You DON'T call me CHLO

He suddenly hugs her. He hasn't done that in a long time. A long pause.

(*Inside the hug.*) WHAT ARE YOU DOING

Joel Sorry.
I'm just trying to brother

Chloe *Brother* then!

Joel I'm trying!

A beat of this holding. To be honest, Chloe is probably relieved.
   Anya comes back into the corridor. Sees them.
   She watches them for a moment.
   Then smirks.

Anya All right then.

Chloe didn't realise she was there.

Fucking hell you guys are so funny.

She moves past them. Looks back.
   Anya goes into the bathroom. For some reason, pops her leg at Chloe as she goes in.
   A sense that the door is locked forever.
   Chloe suddenly pushes Joel off her, furious.

Chloe Fuck I missed it now.

Joel nods a few times, happy though. Like he might have achieved something in his small life.
   After listening for a while, Chloe exits into the living room and Joel off.
   Anya sits beside Mel on the bath.

Anya So.

Mel So.

Anya This then.

Mel I guess

Throughout the next, Anya puts her hand, quite casually, into his trousers. She waits a moment for him to get hard. She starts giving him an efficient handjob.
   She puts his hand into her pants. He starts giving her an ineffective but efficient fingering.
   They stay like this for a while. They don't kiss. It's okay.

Mel struggles to come. He shakes his head, apologetic. He shakes, asking her stop. She does.

He continues fingering Anya. This is all more about concentration and performance than pleasure.

In the living room, Chloe and Jess sit in a fight.
Phoebe has been starting to dry-heave.
She pushes herself onto the floor, to cool her forehead down.
After a while she starts groaning.
They watch her.

Phoebe Oh my god I'm fucked I'm like a fucked girl this is best night off my life

Anya gets bored. She pulls his hand out of her trousers. Hers out of his. After a moment –

Anya That was amaze.

She gets up and starts washing or wiping her hands.

Mel Was it?

A beat. She drops the act –

Anya Oh don't fucking ask that you're so weird

Mel Sorry it doesn't work

Anya looks at him. A smirk.

Anya Yeah.

A beat.

Mel It doesn't work any more

Anya what?

Mel You just don't work any more

A beat.

Anya is it my fault

Mel sort of

Anya what did I do wrong

A beat.

Mel I don't want to say. I think it might upset you.

Anya I am so upset. I am basically upset forever.

Mel This all [all of you, over there] used to work
Honestly
If you were in the room that was all the room was
I mean I wouldn't even listen to anything anyone was saying to me
If you were in the room
No chance
I'd just be – looking over everyone's shoulders at you
Just arrows all out and pointed at all of you
Every second leading up to and during just not letting the ball drop until –

A beat. Elation. Or. No elation?

[One of] you fucked me

A beat.

thank you

A beat.

really, thank you

A beat.

Cos then it was like I just
I dunno
I just
Miraculously
Stopped.

A beat.

Wanting you.

A beat.

I got to stop

A beat. He exhales, free.

I mean. Maybe I just got tired.

Phoebe suddenly jumps up and runs into the bathroom, starts dry-heaving into the toilet.
Mel watches her for a moment. Anya is staring at him.

Or maybe I realised
Maybe I realised
I wasn't looking for you
All that time
I was looking
for My Life
After you

A long beat. Anya is full of the strangest and coldest flame.

You were just in the way

A beat.

Sorry about this but.
You're never beautiful enough, never warm enough.
You're just like I am.
So how can you be so good

Anya suddenly stands up. Overwhelmed. She makes to leave.

Chloe Look. Let's just forgive each other and grow old together.

Anya suddenly turns back, pulls back his head, tries to throw it against the sink, a struggle ensues, her finger is in his mouth. It's quite ungainly and ugly, not elegant.

Jess What?

Chloe Before she comes in let's just. We can still do it. This hasn't all been for nothing.

I know you can't whistle but maybe if we just keep like our hands on each other all night or like grab the bits of each other's tops you know like we used to keep hold of each other's rucksack straps

Anya doesn't manage, even slightly, gives up. He's too strong.
He shakes her off, for the first time actually a bit frightened, a bit out of control.
Mel looks round, realises that Phoebe has been sat bolt upright and is looking back at him.
He looks at her, a little affronted by her stare.
She formulates a question, but doesn't quite get there.
She sinks her head back on the bowl.
He sits on the side of the bath. A little shaken.
Chloe comes out into the hallway. Anya is standing there. A little shaken.
They stand in the corridor.

Anya (*snapping*) What?

Chloe blinks. Smiles.

Chloe So. Did you um.

Anya Yeah.

A beat. Anya is flat and stern.

Chloe Was it good.

A tiny beat.

Anya Sure.

Chloe He's reallyreallyfit.

Anya No he's not.

A beat.

Chloe Oh.

A long pause.

Anya I got up really close and he's like
He's like – fuck-ugly and small
Like you can't tell quality when they're clumped together
They sort of Become more or something
Ha.
But he's just
Really Not Anything

A beat. She doesn't really need to finish that. Maybe that was the finish.

(*Plainly.*) So Yeah I think I'm gonna go now.

Chloe looks at her, mouth agape.

Chloe But – we're about to – go out?
It's
It was midnight wasn't it?

Anya looks at Chloe for a long moment.

Anya No.

Chloe looks bereft. Not understanding.

Come on now.

She gets her stuff together.

She goes into the living room, collects anything left. Jess and her don't look at each other.
For some reason, on exit, she adds, just for Jess –

I didn't fuck him Jess

Jess looks up at her then.

In the hallway – Anya looks at Chloe's face, laughs a little, 'oh babe come on don't be so sad!'
  She smiles.

> *She comes and kisses Chloe on both cheeks. Chloe receives on both cheeks.*
> *Anya faintly glances inside the living room.*
> *And with that, she's gone.*
> *Chloe stands in the hallway for a moment. Bereft.*
> *She slowly walks into the living room.*

After a very long time –

Chloe Yeah I'm going to bed.

Jess looks at her.

Jess Aren't we going out?

Chloe laughs gently, without humour.

Chloe No. We're not going out. Of course we're not *going out*. Of course *we* are not *going out*.

Jess Where's Anya?

Chloe You saw her go did you just want to make me say it ANYA'S GONE and we don't get to

Jess Oh no

Chloe She like fucked him or something and didn't even give a shit and she went. Cos that's what girls get to do they just fuck the guy and then they go and leave us here we have to stay here and they all get to fuck and go.

Jess Where did she go

Chloe I dunno! Not here! Not here any more!

> *Chloe pauses. Her chest is heaving.*
> *Suddenly, softer –*

I don't really want to be here any more? Like these girls? I thought maybe tonight was gonna be the start of us not having to be these girls any more but?
  Obv?
  We can't do that?

She gestures between them; between her and Jess. Her face is a tight little ball.

Chloe So I'm gonna go to bed.

Jess (*sad*) Okay.

She makes to go, turns back, heel of her palm rubbing her eye.

In the hallway, Joel arrives. Outside the living room, listening.

Chloe Look it's sort of hard when you're friends through like all of school since you're in Year Five cos there's not like a time that works to like stop being friends but I think we maybe need to like put one in? Um. I don't want to be those girls any more. I dunno. Yeah. Sorry.
 Do you need to borrow pyjamas?

Jess shakes her head.

Jess (*tiny voice*) No.

Chloe and Jess are still for a moment.

In the bathroom, Phoebe starts trying to pull her top off, or maybe it's her skin, gives up.

Chloe Okay.

Chloe goes.

Chloe passes Joel in the hallway, pretending he's not there.

Jess stands very still for a long moment. She smooths down her skirt, for some reason.
 Tries to decide where to next put her feet.

Mel looks at Phoebe again. She's staring at him.

Mel What? What d'you want?

She sits upright.

Phoebe I'm never having sex

A beat.

Mel Yeah.
Don't.

Phoebe Don't want it don't need it

Mel Me either
Don't even want it. Overrated. Not worth it. Fuck that. Fuck them.

A long beat of nodding at each other. A connection?

Jess turns, realises Joel is standing in the doorway. She jumps a little.

Phoebe So Why you still here then

He looks at her, startled.

if you don't want it

A beat.

Why the Ffuck are you still here.

A beat.

Why the Fuck are you still Here Boy
Why the Fuck are you here

Mel is terrified of her.

Get the Fuck out of us THEN
GET THE FUCK OFF OF US THEN
GET THE FUCK
GET THE FUCK
GET THE FUCK OUT OF US THEN

Mel does – he scuttles out, terrified.
 Phoebe lies her head back on the toilet.

yeah

Joel I'm sorry

Jess suddenly walks over to Joel and presses her lips to his.
He presses back, but barely. He is terrified, paralysed. Every particle of his body is alight. He is torn between passivity and a demonstration of the intense overwhelming feelings he holds for her.
He almost implodes with the pressure of the interaction between these two things. A little, desperate, needing, human noise erupts from his mouth.
Jess suddenly finishes the kiss. She moves her head back, just a little. She bows her head, eyes closed. They both cannot look at each other.

(*Barely audible.*) You'resobeautiful.

Jess What?

Joel I said You're beautiful. You're so beautiful

Jess Oh.

Joel Jess.

Jess Oh.

A pause.

Joel (*barely audible*) You're so beautiful Jess and I love you.

Jess can't answer.

Jess Oh my god I.
You.
But I also, do. that. Um

A long connecting pause.

Phoebe fuck 'em all I'll never

They suddenly spontaneously kiss again, a peck, equal. They do not touch each other with their hands.

They smile at each other.
They could just as easily cry.
The lovers kiss again, a little longer. They separate and smile at each other.
A long pause, gazing.

Joel (*laughingly*) I – don't know what to do now!

A bit of giggling.
They kiss again, and Joel brings his hands behind her head. She brings her hands to his sides.
They separate, smiling lightly, drunk on the moment.
Joel, still smiling, still holding on to the back of her head, twists her around and lays her front onto the back of the armchair, so she is bent over in front of him.
The sudden movement provokes surprise but not objection in her.
He gently brings her arms behind her back, and holds her hands there behind her back. He then releases her hands and she keeps them there.
He doesn't know what to do for a moment, he looks down at her quite passively.
She doesn't know what to do, so she waits.
He pulls down her trousers a little. He again anticipates objection but none comes.

(*Tiny tiny voice.*) Yeah?

A brief pause.

Jess (*tiny tiny voice*) Yeah?

He pulls down his trousers and puts himself inside her.
She makes a small sound of discomfort and pain and he stops.
Then she is silent.
He starts gently fucking her.
They have consensual sex.

Joel I love you

Jess I love you

After a while, she starts making Phoebe's porn sound.
That faint moan.
This happens for a bit.
Lights fall.
A bit of time in the dark.
The pair sit on the sofa, holding hands.
They're both in love.
They're both in shock.
It's the end of something.

Joel Is it over now

Lights fall.
End of play.